blueberry
pancakes
forever

blueberry
pancakes
forever

angelica
banks

ALLEN&UNWIN
SYDNEY·MELBOURNE·AUCKLAND·LONDON

First published by Allen & Unwin in 2016

Allen & Unwin
83 Alexander Street
Crows Nest NSW 2065
Australia
Phone: (61 2) 8425 0100
Email: info@allenandunwin.com
Web: www.allenandunwin.com

A Cataloguing-in-Publication entry is available from the
National Library of Australia
www.trove.nla.gov.au

ISBN 978 1 76011 045 1

Author photo: © *The Mercury*, Hobart
Cover & text design by Design by Committee
Cover illustration: Josh Durham
Typeset by Midland Typesetters, Australia

P

I

w

For BAFFIX

Nothing you can imagine
is ever truly lost

In honour of good fathers
everywhere, including ours

And in memory of Isla
who loved to read

Chapter One

This is how it is when winter falls. The sun rises, but a little later than it did yesterday and a little earlier than it will tomorrow. Each night is longer, darker and colder than the one before.

Back at the beginning of winter, Vivienne Small had lined her hammock with fur and covered herself at night with an extra blanket. She had collected wood to burn in the pot-belly stove on her verandah, and spent the long evenings sitting close beside it, whispering to her black rat Ermengarde about the things they would do when springtime came. But although weeks passed, and months too, the winter did not turn. Instead it grew steadily deeper.

The snow on the Mountains of Margalov crept lower and lower, and the upper reaches of the River of Rythwyck turned to ice. The Golden Valley was no longer golden but white, and the five Cities of Luminosity were buried beneath snowdrifts. Plants no longer grew, but instead lay dormant beneath the frosty earth. Hibernating animals slept on and on. The birds of the air laid no eggs; chrysalises never broke open. The creatures of the world were starving, and Vivienne could do nothing but watch as the world inched closer to complete and absolute darkness.

On a particularly bitter morning, Vivienne woke beneath a pile of blankets, a woollen hat pulled down over her ears. Despite her coverings, she was cold and the tip of her nose was numb. The only pool of warmth was at the back of her neck, where Ermengarde was asleep beneath Vivienne's dark, tangled hair.

Vivienne sat up and opened her wide blue wings, releasing a shower of ice crystals. Ermengarde emerged briefly, squinted disapprovingly at the morning, and retreated once again. Vivienne shook the ice off her long leather boots and pulled them stiffly onto her feet. She wrapped her arms about herself tightly as she stood at the railing of her verandah, and stared out over the angry charcoal waves of the Restless Sea. The sky above was no friendlier.

The long and terrible winter had begun with an earthquake that had shaken every tree in the Peppermint Forest from the depths of their roots to the tips of their leaves. It had caused giant waves to crash against the shores, eating away at cliffs and scouring the sand from beaches. It had ruptured hills and valleys, and reduced parts of the City of Clocks to rubble. Then winter had come, and had not departed. There was speculation in every wild and tame place, among strangers and friends, that the world had been shaken so violently it had come loose from the turning of its seasons. Many said spring would never come again, and that the winter would deepen, day by day, until it had frozen the entire world and everything in it.

For a long while, Vivienne had scoffed at such an idea. But as the weeks unravelled, growing ever darker and colder, a tiredness had stolen over her. She had begun to wonder if winter was here forever, and this truly was the end of the world as she had known it. She leaned wearily on the railing and her stomach growled. But there was no point even looking in her pantry. She and Ermengarde had shared the last of her final store of nuts and a remnant of dry cheese two days ago. She had long since visited her other homes and stores, bringing any remaining supplies back to the Peppermint Forest, and now her tree house was completely empty of anything edible. She shivered.

'It's about time we had some sunshine!' she called to the invisible sun, trapped behind layers of stormy clouds. 'This can't go on *forever*!'

'Forever is a long time,' came an eerie, otherworldly voice from behind her. 'A long, long time.'

Vivienne caught the scent of dank earth, but before she could turn to see who had spoken, she felt in her shoulder the sharp stab of a dart. She saw a flash of vibrant green, then her knees buckled and everything faded to black.

Chapter Two

Along a rocky stretch of coastline, where cliffs soared to the sky and seabirds soared even higher, there stood a lighthouse. Perched on a grim knuckle of stone, it was the loneliest of places, lucky to be visited by two or three ships each year. And yet, on this particular day, it was surrounded by a flotilla of fishing boats. On their decks were photographers and reporters with their camera lenses trained on the red door of the lighthouse. Right on midday, it opened.

Out of the lighthouse stepped a woman dressed in a vivid blue coat and carrying a bucket.

The buffeting wind made her long red hair fly about as if in a blender. The long skirts of her coat flew up, revealing a pair of spectacular red boots. After waving to the assembly of fishing boats, the woman made her way along a rough, sloping path that led to the water's edge where she crouched to carefully fill her bucket. That done, she caught up a thick cable of rope and began to haul on it, hand over hand.

The fishing boats attempted to edge closer, but the crashing waves and maze of half-submerged rocks deterred even the most valiant skippers. Several of the journalists put megaphones to their mouths and began calling questions over the wind:

'Serendipity, can you tell us what you're writing?'

'Serendipity, is Vivienne Small going to feature in the new series?'

'Serendipity, when are you coming back to the city?'

'Serendipity, do you know that *Vivienne Small and the Final Battle* is now the best-selling children's novel of all time?'

'The Mirage Hotel is keen to have you back. They're asking do you need crème brûlée shipped in?'

'Serendipity, do you have a message for your young readers?'

But Serendipity simply waved, and when at last the lobster pot she had been hauling in emerged at the end of the rope, she inspected its contents. Rolling back her sleeve, she plunged in her hand and brought out a marvellous orange-speckled lobster, its arms and legs waving like those of a space monster. She held it aloft for a moment and imagined the flurry and whirr of equipment as the media captured this image and sent it around the world.

Then she lowered the lobster into her water-filled bucket and clipped on the lid. Walking more slowly this time, and leaning slightly from the weight of the bucket, she made her way back to the lighthouse. At seventeen minutes past midday, she gave a final wave to the assembled fleet, then disappeared inside.

Several of the journalists shook their heads.

'We *must* be able to get onto the island,' one said to the ship's captain.

'Not likely,' the captain replied, shrugging her shoulders and shaking her head. 'It's simply impossible to visit until we can send a rowboat across, and that is only possible on the lowest of tides.'

'Well, when will that happen?'

'They come once a year. The next one's only six weeks away.'

'Six weeks! We can't wait *six weeks*.'

'Take it up with the moon,' the captain said.

The journalist thought for a moment, stared up at the dull grey sky that showed neither sun nor moon, and sighed.

'She's been out here alone for months and months,' he mused, trying a different tack. 'It must be hard for her, not having anyone to talk to.'

'She speaks to Constanza, by radio,' said the captain, with a wry smile.

Constanza was the proprietor of the only shop in the tiny village that clung to the mainland's cliffs and overlooked the lighthouse. It was Constanza who took Serendipity's weekly grocery order and organised the helicopter to make the delivery.

'Constanza is hardly a conversationalist,' the reporter said. He had used every tactic imaginable to convince the taciturn Constanza to let him travel on the helicopter, or at the very least use the shop radio to contact Serendipity at the lighthouse. But with no success.

'Have you considered that maybe Ms Smith doesn't want to talk to you?' said the captain.

'But surely she misses her fans?' the reporter said.

'My own mother was a writer,' said the captain, somewhat wistfully. 'She used to say that you could never be lonely with your characters beside you.'

'So that's it? She won't come out again until … until when?'

The captain shrugged.

'There's got to be something we can do,' the journalist said. 'The whole world is desperate for news!'

'Well,' said the skipper with a sigh, 'if you want to, you can pay me and we'll sit here all day, every day, watching and waiting. It's your money. But I assure you, she's gone for today.'

And so, one by one, the fishing boats turned away from the lighthouse and made their way back to the village in the distance.

On the rocky outcrop the wind continued to blow, whistling through a narrow crack under the lighthouse door, and between the windowpanes. Inside, a red wig lay in a tangle on a table and the electric blue coat had been hung on a peg. The red boots had been unlaced and discarded.

At the sink stood Miss Digby in a pair of sheepskin boots, her usually tidy hair ever so slightly dishevelled from being tucked up under the wig. Through the thick glass of the narrow window, she watched the retreating fishing boats. Each day, they were edging closer, becoming bolder. She knew they'd eventually find a way onto the island. That simply wouldn't do. She could lock the door, but sooner or later, she'd have to come out and face their probing lenses and endless questions.

Miss Digby shuddered at the thought, then turned her attention to the bucket in the sink. She removed the lid and was greeted by a host of coral-coloured claws and legs, all waving.

'I am sorry, Gerald,' she said as she gingerly lifted the lobster out of the bucket and lowered him into a large aquarium tank full of seawater. 'I know it's inconvenient, but you needn't fear. We both know the drill.'

Gerald landed on the pebbles on the floor of the tank and scuttled behind a large frond of seaweed. There, he would hunker down, in a mild sulk, until darkness fell and Miss Digby would pop him back into his bucket, walk down to the shore and release him into the sea. They had been through this catch-and-release routine every few days since the media had discovered her whereabouts. Miss Digby thought Gerald would have learned to avoid the lobster pot, but it seemed that he found her oyster and tuna baits irresistible. Truth be told, she was grateful for his company, even if he was given to sulking.

Miss Digby fixed herself a cup of tea and a cheese-and-pickled-onion sandwich. She ate, all the while feeling troubled. When she was done, she walked a circle around the tiny room, then slumped into a chair beside the aquarium and peered into its watery gloom.

'Why isn't she answering my calls, Gerald?' Miss Digby said. 'Gerald? *Gerald?*'

But there was no reply.

Miss Digby sighed and reached for the radio. Not that she expected to get much more of a response from the radio than she did from the moping crustacean. She cleared her throat and, in her best Serendipity Smith voice, said, 'Good afternoon. Constanza, are you there?'

'*Sí,*' came a flat voice.

'Constanza, I wonder could you try the Brown Street number again?'

'*Sí,* Senora Smith,' said Constanza, pronouncing it *Smeet.*

Miss Digby could hear the phone ringing. The ringing went on and on and on. But no one answered. She sighed.

'I'll try again tomorrow, Constanza,' said

Miss Digby, trying to not sound too despondent. '*Gracias.*'

'*Adiós*, Senora *Smeet*,' said Constanza.

It had been more than three months since Miss Digby had spoken to the woman she was impersonating, the world's most famous author Serendipity Smith, and longer still since she had seen her in person. For a year now, Serendipity had been out of contact with the world. Although requests continued to pour in from schools and libraries, bookstores and television shows, for visits and interviews, everyone who sought Serendipity's attention received the same response:

Thank you for contacting Serendipity Smith! At present, Serendipity is busy creating a new series of books. She is unable to give any interviews or attend any public events during this time. She thanks her readers for their patience and hopes they are continuing to discover many wonderful stories, both in their own lives and in the books they read.

As well as impersonating Serendipity, Miss Digby was managing the famous writer's affairs by correspondence. Each week by helicopter, along with groceries, there came a huge pile of redirected mail carefully packed in cardboard boxes. From the bank statements, Miss Digby could tell that Serendipity was hardly leaving the house. There were sporadic home deliveries of pizzas, noodles and curries. But there were no shopping trips or books or movie tickets. Surely Tuesday had needed shoes when school had resumed? Had there really been no trips to the museum, no afternoons of ice-skating or new winter coats?

Miss Digby thought again of the phone ringing on and on in the hallway at Brown Street. Once, that hallway had always smelled of something freshly baked. With a troubled sigh, she wondered what it smelled of now.

14

Chapter Three

It was winter and the branches of the trees that lined Brown Street were entirely bare. Although the sun had been up and about for a few hours, little patches of the night's frost lingered in the shadows on the ground. In the middle of Brown Street, the McGillycuddy place was as tall and narrow as ever. And yet the house appeared altered. As if it had lost confidence and no longer wanted to be seen.

It had the same number of steps leading up to the front door, the same number of storeys, and the same number of windows, including the single large window on the very top floor. As you know, that large top-floor window looked into the writing room of the most famous writer in the world. Very few people knew this fact, however, because Serendipity Smith preferred to spend most of her life as an ordinary woman called Sarah McGillycuddy.

One long year had passed since the last of her Vivienne Small books had been published, and it was longer still since Serendipity Smith had announced that she was starting work on a new adventure series. The days and weeks and months had slipped by, but no new book had appeared, and readers were getting impatient.

Had you been able to peer in through the window of Serendipity's writing room, you would have seen very little to reassure you that the first book in Serendipity Smith's new series was on its way to your local bookshop. On one side of Serendipity's desk there was a huge stack of blank paper. And although there was a page threaded through Serendipity's big antique typewriter, if you were to look closely, you would see that it had been there long enough to gather dust, and that not a single word was written upon it.

There was also a fine layer of dust on the typewriter keys, on the stack of blank paper, and on the lid of a little silver box that Serendipity kept on her desk.

The air in the writing room had a stale smell. This had to do with the dust and also with a cup of long-ago tea that had been left – back in the days when it was half full, and not half empty – to slowly moulder on Serendipity's desk. But the smell had more to do with the fact that no one had been in the room for a very long time. For months nobody had sat down in the big red velvet chair to read, and nobody had selected a volume from the shelves that were stacked, floor to ceiling, with books of every imaginable kind. Nobody had sat down at the desk to stare out the window, no one had thrown the window wide, and no story had trailed its silver thread in or out. In that room there had been no writing: not of the dreaming kind, nor of the hammering-on-the-keyboard kind, and not even of the pen-on-paper kind.

And nor would Serendipity Smith do any writing on this particular Saturday. Though it was after ten o'clock, she was still in bed. She was quite awake, but lying very still with the covers pulled right up under her chin. The phone had been ringing, but she had let it ring out. She was watching the numbers on her bedside clock as they slowly ticked over. She should get up and start the day, she thought, but somehow she lacked the strength. Five more minutes, she decided. Yes, just five.

Of course, Serendipity Smith wasn't the only writer in residence at Brown Street. The other one was Tuesday McGillycuddy, Serendipity's daughter. But Tuesday wasn't writing either. She was curled up in the corner of the couch in the living room, still in her pyjamas. She and her dog Baxterr were watching television. At least, they were sitting together staring at a screen upon which colours changed and people moved, and from which there came the occasional burst of fake laughter. If you had asked either girl or dog what the program was about, they would not have been able to say.

Upstairs in Tuesday's room, Tuesday's baby blue typewriter had been moved from its position in the middle of her desk and shoved under the bed. Also under the bed were several scrunched-up items of school uniform, a pair of broken ice skates and an old suitcase containing all the pages Tuesday had so far written about her adventures. This suitcase had not been opened for a long time.

Even though it was Saturday, and past ten o'clock, there was no sign of breakfast being prepared in the kitchen. The grill of the once spotless oven was strung with drips of burnt-black cheese. There were dark splashes of sauce congealed on the stovetop. The dishwasher had been abandoned after its filter had clogged some months ago, and the clock on the wall was now permanently stopped at a quarter to three, but whether that was A.M. or P.M. was anybody's guess.

The door to the laundry had not been opened for weeks. Behind it was a waiting tsunami of unwashed sheets and towels and tea towels and socks, poised to overtake the whole house. In the living room, as well as in the downstairs bathroom, there were candle stubs and empty matchboxes lying around, because various light globes had blown some time ago. It seemed, at

Brown Street, as if all the regular household activities of cleaning, mending, washing, organising and tidying up had been suspended indefinitely. But that wasn't the worst of it. There was also the fact that the house felt cold, no matter how much Tuesday turned up the heating. And then there was the way it sounded. You could listen at the keyhole all day if you wanted to, and you still wouldn't hear a giggle or a laugh.

Perhaps you've already guessed why. It's because there was someone missing. That someone was Denis McGillycuddy. And he wasn't ever coming back.

Tuesday's father had died on a Friday in the City Hospital while Serendipity held one of his hands and Tuesday held the other. The tumour that had affected his head the year before had returned, and no matter how hard they had tried, doctors had not been able to fix the things that had gone wrong with Denis's body.

Serendipity and Tuesday knew that Denis wouldn't have wanted his funeral to be a sad affair. So there had been jokes, and poems, wonderful speeches, several funny songs and even a tongue-twister competition which had no clear winner because no one could say *the sixth sick sheik's sixth sheep's sick* without stumbling, although everyone knew that Denis would have been able to. Everybody had tried to be cheerful, but of course nobody had succeeded.

For the first few weeks after Denis died, the phone at Brown Street rang often with people calling to tell Tuesday and her mother that they were thinking of them, and to ask if there was anything they could do, which there wasn't. Tuesday and Serendipity found casseroles and soups, banana bread and oatmeal cookies on their front doorstep, left there by friends, neighbours and people from Tuesday's school who wanted to show they cared. During the early weeks after Denis died, Tuesday ate so much pumpkin soup that now pumpkin soup, to Tuesday, tasted of tears.

Then the phone calls and the pumpkin soup eased off. For a while Miss Digby had taken care of everything. But it soon became clear that Miss Digby was also required to dress up as Serendipity Smith, go out into the world, and keep up the impression that all was well with the world's most famous writer.

This was not, however, a perfect solution, because although it was easy for Miss Digby to be Serendipity at a distance, it was impossible for her to do interviews or television appearances. Anyone with a sharp eye would notice the many small differences between the two women, despite all the distractions of glasses and wigs, coloured contact lenses and fabulous coats. Miss Digby's voice was a different timbre and accent to Serendipity's, and her manner could never quite match the authority that came so naturally to the real Serendipity Smith. So after some months, Miss Digby decided it was time for the public Serendipity to go on a long holiday, far from the city and the Hotel Mirage and all the places she usually frequented.

'But where *will* you go?' Serendipity had asked.

'The end of the earth seems appropriate,' Miss Digby said drily.

Now a whole year had passed, and Tuesday's teachers had long since stopped asking her if she needed more time to complete her homework, and her friends had forgotten to try not to mention – on Monday mornings – all the great things they'd done with their fathers over the weekend. People were getting on with their lives. But for Serendipity, Baxterr and Tuesday, life was utterly different and getting on with it seemed impossible.

Sometimes things appeared almost normal. Tuesday woke up in the mornings and had a shower and put on her school uniform and ate breakfast and went to school and came home in the afternoons and watched television and ate dinner and brushed her teeth and went to bed with Baxterr beside her. And then she did it all again the next day. On the weekends, she slept and watched more television. And quite often she managed to take Baxterr for a walk. But all the time and energy she might have had left over for doing anything else was used up in trying to keep herself away from a particular feeling. It wasn't simply the unbearable absence of her

23

father in the house, or missing the food he no longer cooked, the games he no longer played, the books they no longer talked about, or the ideas he no longer shared. It was as if at the core of everything, including herself and her mother, there was a gaping hole.

'Ruff,' said Baxterr to Tuesday when the television program finished.

'What's that, doggo?' Tuesday asked, with a yawn.

'Hurrrrrrr,' he said.

'Yes, all right. I suppose I could eat something too. Let's go see what there is.'

In the kitchen Tuesday opened the fridge and sighed. She remembered when the fridge had been brimming with eggs and milk and fresh vegetables and seven or eight types of cheese. Now there was only a carton of long-life milk, a bunch of limp baby carrots, a rind of parmesan cheese and some butter with a use-by date of six months ago.

'Come on. Let's go and get Mum out of

bed. We'll take her out for breakfast. Again,' Tuesday said.

Baxterr hung his shaggy golden-brown head and Tuesday bent to ruffle his fur.

'Oh, doggo. It'll be fun. Really. There's that new cafe. We haven't tried *there* yet. Maybe today's our day. Maybe it's the one!'

But, looking into her dog's sad brown eyes, Tuesday could see that Baxterr wasn't any more hopeful than she was.

Within the hour a girl in a red coat, a dog on a loose lead, and a woman in a black coat and woollen hat set off down Brown Street in the direction of City Park. The city was full of cafes, and when Denis had been alive, going out for breakfast had been a treat. Now, it had become more of a necessity.

Tuesday, Serendipity and Baxterr had discovered a florist cafe where the tables and chairs were squeezed in between huge earthenware vases full of pink and white lilies. But even before they got to the blueberry pancakes, Tuesday had begun sneezing. There was also a laundry cafe where huge, old-fashioned washing machines hummed and spun – full of clothes and bright white suds – while people ate and drank. But the blueberry pancakes there were rubbery. And there was a cafe that belonged to an artist who had painted murals on the walls, the tables, the chairs and ceiling as well. The pictures she made were so real that Tuesday always felt as if she could fall into their scenes. But the blueberry pancakes never had enough blueberries and the maple syrup was fake.

The cafe they planned to try this day was called Crème Brûlée.

'That has to be a good sign, doesn't it, Mum?' Tuesday asked Serendipity, trying as hard as she could to sound cheerful. 'Crème brûlée? Your favourite?'

'What? Oh, yes, crème brûlée,' said Serendipity, trying to appear attentive when Tuesday knew she was a million miles away. 'My favourite.'

The cafe had a parquetry floor and glass cabinets full of cakes and pastries. Serendipity and Tuesday took a small table near the window and Baxterr lay in a patch of sunshine on the floor beside them. Tuesday and Serendipity ordered blueberry pancakes. Tuesday also ordered a not-too-hot hot chocolate, and Serendipity a strong coffee.

'Well, they're not rubbery,' Tuesday said, when the pancakes arrived.

'No,' Serendipity agreed, taking a mouthful.

'And there are plenty of blueberries,' Tuesday admitted. 'But ...'

She and her mother looked at each other.

'... they're just not the same,' Serendipity finished.

Chapter Four

Later that Saturday, Tuesday and Serendipity were at the kitchen table playing Scrabble. Although it was mid-afternoon, the game they had started when they'd come home from breakfast was only about halfway done. Tuesday had made some nice words like *antique* and *ivory* and *sorbet*, but Serendipity had struggled to make even simple words like *flat* and *leaf* and *vale*. It was Serendipity's turn, but Tuesday suspected her mother might actually have forgotten. Tuesday didn't want to nag her, so she yawned and stretched, looked at the clock that was stuck on a quarter to three, pushed her toes silently against the floor, and waited.

She felt as if she had been waiting for something to happen for weeks. She had even considered whether she should make something happen herself, but the dreadful fatigue that dogged her days and nights never quite let her get up enough steam. She wondered if she should go to the shops and buy food to cook for an early dinner, considering they'd forgotten to have lunch. But the only thing she knew how to cook was pasta with bottled sauce, and she was bored with that. Maybe she could build a card house? Or play Patience? But, no. She couldn't remember where the playing cards were.

Then, suddenly, startlingly, something did happen. The doorbell rang, long and loud and insistent. It woke Baxterr. He leapt to his feet and hurtled out into the hallway while Serendipity and Tuesday stared at each other, puzzled, as if they too were awakening from a dream.

Serendipity said, 'They'll go away.'

Tuesday nodded. They had played this game before, avoiding the ringing telephone, sitting quietly while people knocked and buzzed and rang. It felt peculiar to hide in your own house, but that was the only way they could avoid the conversations people always wanted to have.

After a moment or two, the doorbell rang again, even louder and for quite a lot longer. Serendipity looked pained. Then the doorbell rang again and whoever was outside did not take their finger off the button.

'I'll go,' Tuesday said. 'They might be selling something. I'll just tell them we're not interested.'

'Would you?' Serendipity said with a sigh of relief. 'I'm not here. Whoever they are. Okay?'

With Baxterr at her ankles, Tuesday opened the door. Outside was a woman wearing a huge coat made from fur that might recently have belonged to a grizzly bear. A pair of sunglasses was pushed up on her unruly blonde hair. She observed Tuesday with intense curiosity. Tuesday, in turn, took in the woman's keen gaze, her faded shirt and pants, and her lace-up boots that looked as if they had survived a trek across the Andes and then tackled the Himalayas (which in fact they had). At her feet was a fleet of matching silver suitcases.

'Tuesday?' asked the woman in a gravelly, accented voice.

'Yes,' said Tuesday.

'I'm Colette Baden-Baden. Is your mother home?'

'Well,' said Tuesday, and although she had been about to say *no*, she found she couldn't lie to this woman. 'It's not a good time.'

The woman pursed her lips. 'I know. I understand. Tell her ... tell her that Colette is here.'

'Um ...' said Tuesday. But before she could say any more, Serendipity appeared behind her in the hallway.

'Colette?' Serendipity was staring as if she were seeing a ghost. 'Is it really you?'

'I came as soon as I heard. I know, I know. Terribly late. But here I am.'

And then the two woman were embracing and the embrace continued for a very long, silent moment before Colette stepped back and said, 'Well, then. As bad as that. Hmm. Thought as much.'

The next moment, Colette and Tuesday were carrying suitcases and Baxterr was wagging his tail and following them all down the hallway. Back in the kitchen, Tuesday swept the Scrabble set away into its box without a second thought. Serendipity absently filled the kettle and then forgot to light the stove. Colette lit the stove, washed three cups from the pile in the sink, and found in the pantry an almost-but-not-quite empty packet of tea-leaves. She patted Serendipity on the shoulder and nodded to Tuesday, and this resulted in both Serendipity and Tuesday sitting down as if they were the visitors in their own kitchen.

When at last the tea was made and served, Colette said, 'Tea is very good for sadness, but maybe not quite good enough.'

From one of the pockets of her great fur coat, she extracted a green glass bottle. She dropped a dash of its contents into all three teacups. Tuesday lifted her cup to her nose and took a sniff, then a sip. The taste was curiously warming, as if the tea had been spiked with chillies and cinnamon. Almost instantly she felt a pleasant shiver run through her. She saw the same thing happen to her mother.

Colette gazed from mother to daughter.

'I cannot tell you how good it is to see you both. Nor how sorry I am, how very sorry I am, unspeakably sorry, about Denis. I'm sure you've both been through the worst year of your lives. Whatever I can do, however I can help, I'm here. If you need me to stay, I can. Or if you need to not have visitors, I'm happy to go.'

'You can stay?' asked Serendipity.

Colette nodded. 'As long as you need.'

Serendipity turned to Tuesday. 'Would you mind, Tuesday? If Colette were to stay for a while?'

Tuesday scrunched her eyebrows together in the way she did when she was thinking hard. 'Yes, I think you should stay,' she said to Colette. 'But I seem to be missing something. I don't know who you are.'

'Yes, you do,' said Serendipity. 'She's your godmother.'

'Oh,' said Tuesday. '*That* Colette.'

Tuesday stared at Colette in a way that might have bordered on rude, but Colette didn't seem to mind. Tuesday thought that Colette didn't look the least bit like the godmother she had imagined. All the postcards, erratic presents and late-night phone calls that her parents had taken had given her an idea of someone more like an airline hostess.

'Officially appointed at your birth,' said Colette. 'Gave you three wishes. Protected you against the bad fairies. Only allowed the good ones. At least, I think that's how it went. It was quite a party, your naming day. Then, when you were only two, I went off on this project. I've been travelling the world for more than ten years making a documentary. That's what I do, did you know? I'm a filmmaker. Alaska, Africa, India, South America, Antarctica. I've been a terrible godmother. I don't think I have ever even sent you a card within two months of your birthday.'

'It doesn't matter,' said Tuesday and Serendipity together.

'Of course it matters,' said Colette. 'But I assumed you were growing up perfectly well and I wasn't needed. I mean, that's what godmothers are for, aren't they? To arrive when needed.

34

Well, I've done badly there, too, because I'm more than a year too late.'

She glanced about, sniffed the air as if she were measuring the likelihood of rain inside the house, and said, 'Yes. Far too late. The one title anyone ever gave me in life that I hadn't expected – *godmother* – and I've made a mess of it.'

'Not necessarily,' said Tuesday, with a grin. 'Maybe this is exactly when you're meant to arrive.'

Colette considered Tuesday with her deep brown eyes and, in that moment, Tuesday understood that Colette Baden-Baden was one of those people who smile with their eyes.

'I remember you when you were first born,' Colette said. 'You liked me to carry you over my shoulder. Went to sleep there, when not much else worked. I've still got photographs and films from back then. I will get them out.'

Tuesday wanted to ask so many questions. How did her parents know Colette? Was that actually a bearskin she was wearing? Did Colette know her mother was also the world's most famous author, Serendipity Smith, creator of the Vivienne Small series?

'I am very good at keeping secrets,' Colette said, winking at Tuesday. 'I know when to call your mother Sarah and when to call her Serendipity.'

Tuesday was startled. Had Colette Baden-Baden read her thoughts?

Serendipity, seeing the expression on Tuesday's face, began to explain. 'Colette went to school with your father. In fact they lived next door to each other from when they were very young.'

'We got expelled,' said Colette. 'Together.'

Colette and Serendipity smirked at each other.

'His fault you got caught,' said Serendipity.

'My idea to do it in the first place,' said Colette.

Colette looked at Tuesday. 'We must become friends.'

'Okay,' said Tuesday. The warmth of the tea had reached her toes and she was feeling pleasantly light-headed. There was something highly irregular about Colette. It was partly in the way she sat: very upright, as if she wasn't used to chairs with backs. It was also in the low growl of her

36

voice, and the way she pronounced words with the emphasis in unexpected places. And it was in the steady way she took everything in, almost as if she were on guard, ready to defend herself at a moment's notice.

Colette poured more tea and added more of her special potion. When the teapot was empty and the small green bottle completely drained, Colette announced they were all going out for hamburgers. Baxterr ate a Cuban sandwich, which he thought was the nearest thing to dog paradise you could get in this world. Tuesday saw her mother smile more times in a single hour than she had done since Denis fell ill. It was late when they returned to Brown Street. In the hallway, Tuesday kissed Serendipity (who hugged her fiercely) and hugged Colette (who kissed her fiercely), and went upstairs, with Baxterr, to bed.

Alone together Colette and Serendipity smiled at each other in the manner of the old, old friends they were.

'I'm so glad you're here,' Serendipity said. 'We could talk all night and still have too much to say. But it's late. I should make a bed for you.'

'Just show me to a room,' Colette said. 'Any room. The laundry will do.'

'Not possible,' said Serendipity.

Colette, with a suitcase in either hand and refusing any assistance from Serendipity, followed Serendipity up, and up, and up to the writing room on the top floor.

'Hmm,' said Colette, looking about. She gravitated towards the bookshelves, nodding as she recognised the titles of many of the books that were crammed right way up, upside down and sideways into the shelves that covered the walls.

'It's a bit … oh, I'm sorry,' Serendipity said, noticing the mouldy cup of tea and whisking it up, causing a small dust storm as she did so. 'This room could do with a good clean.'

'Tomorrow,' said Colette. 'We might wash a little of the sadness out of this whole house, hmmm?'

'Is it time?' Serendipity asked.

Colette nodded.

'There's a spare mattress—' Serendipity began.

'No need,' Colette said, and proceeded to unsnap the latches of one of the silver cases. She drew out of it a long thin drawstring bag that held silver poles of the extendable sort you might use to put up a tent. Serendipity sank into her big, deep-red velvet reading chair and watched as Colette joined the poles into a frame that she finished with the addition of two large hooks at either end. Then she whipped out a hammock and hung each of its loops onto the hooks.

'There,' she said, with a grin. 'Instant bed.'

'I thought you might have gotten softer in your old age,' said Serendipity.

'Ha! Couldn't sleep on a mattress, even if I wanted to. Spongy. Like sleeping on a strudel,' Colette said.

Although she was a tall woman, Colette was nimble as she clambered into her hammock.

'Can I get you a quilt, or a pillow?'

'Bah!' said Colette. 'I don't believe in them.'

She lay down, crossed her ankles and pulled her fur coat about her.

'Thank you for coming,' Serendipity said. 'We need you. Tuesday needs you. I haven't been much use since ...'

'Hmm,' Colette said, in a way that seemed to suggest that all of this might be true, but nevertheless, it was the best that could be expected. 'She's a good girl that one. She's just what you would expect to get if you put you and Denis in a food processor and whizzed you about.'

Serendipity winced a little at the thought.

'But with a dash of magic, too. She's creative, yes?'

'Very,' said Serendipity. 'Though not so much ... lately.'

'And then there's Baxterr,' Colette continued, her gravelly accent giving extra dimensions to the double R. 'He is not a regular dog, is he? Where on earth did you find him?'

Serendipity gave her old friend a wan smile. 'You've always seen things that nobody else does, haven't you?'

'Hmm,' agreed Colette. 'And since you speak of seeing things, what on earth is that?'

Colette was pointing beyond Serendipity's

writing desk and typewriter to the drawn curtains at the window.

'What?' asked Serendipity.

'*That*,' Colette insisted, sitting suddenly upright in her hammock.

And then Serendipity saw it, easing its way in through the opening where the two curtains overlapped. It was a fine filament of thread, and it was drifting further into the room, curling in soft loops in the air above the typewriter, making its way unmistakably towards Serendipity.

'It's ... er ...' Serendipity stammered.

'Purple,' suggested Colette. 'Or would you call that violet?'

'Mauve?' suggested Serendipity, who in all her life as a writer had never seen thread that wasn't silver.

'That is most unusual,' Colette said.

'It is,' Serendipity agreed.

Colette leapt out of her hammock and peered at the thread, her brow furrowed. And as she watched, the thread twined itself around the index finger of Serendipity's outstretched hand.

'This is a writing thing, yes?' Colette said.

Serendipity nodded. 'It's a ... story. Well, it might be. You know, the beginning of one.'

'Curious,' said Colette.

'But I have nothing to write,' said Serendipity, partly to Colette, but mostly to the thread.

'Still, it has come for you, yes?' Colette asked.

'It has.' The thread was winding about Serendipity's wrists and tangling around her ankles. 'But I can't. It has to stop.'

She set about shooing the thread away, but this only seemed to encourage it.

'I can't possibly leave Tuesday,' she said. 'Or ...' and the word *Denis* hung in the air unsaid, though they both heard it.

Colette thought for a moment. 'So, if you go, will you be gone long?'

'It's difficult to say,' Serendipity said. 'Not usually. Often I'm back by morning.'

'It would be good for you to go, don't you think?' asked Colette.

'I don't know,' said Serendipity. 'I'm not sure I'm ready.'

'I think you'd better go. In my experience stories do not wait until we think we're ready.'

The thread was winding around Serendipity's middle and lifting her out of her chair. Colette watched in amazement as Serendipity now floated above her desk.

'So that is how it happens,' Colette said. 'Ha. I have lived to see another remarkable thing.'

An invisible wind blew back the curtains and the large window opened to the night sky like an invitation. Serendipity let out a laugh.

'Go, my friend,' said Colette. 'I will take care of your beloved Tuesday until you return. I promise.'

'I'll be back as quickly as I can,' said Serendipity.

'Everyone here will be safe. You have my word,' said Colette.

With what seemed to Colette to be alarming speed, Serendipity was drawn out of the window and up into the star-filled night. For a moment, she was still visible to the astonished Colette. And then, all of a sudden, she was not.

Chapter Five

The following morning, Tuesday woke with a start, feeling as if she had slept more deeply than she had for weeks. With a sigh of relief, she remembered it was Sunday. There was the sound of rain falling outside and she was about to remark upon this to Baxterr when she saw that he was already gone from the foot of her bed where he usually slept.

Making her way down the stairs, she could hear the gruff voice of Colette Baden-Baden, rising and falling in a one-sided conversation. Tuesday pushed open the kitchen door to find Baxterr sitting on a chair across the table from Colette, his head cocked, his eyes imploring her.

'I already told you, Baxterr, I do not make pancakes,' Colette was saying, waving a finger at him. 'No, no. No pancakes. In my world there is muesli or toast. Sometimes chilli beans. Sometimes fresh fish. Or eggs. But no bothersome pancakes.'

'Good morning,' said Tuesday.

Colette spun around. 'Well, good morning to you, Tuesday. Did you sleep well?'

'Yes, I did, thank you,' said Tuesday. 'Are you really talking to Baxterr?'

'Of course,' said Colette. 'He is trying to convince me to cook pancakes.'

'How do you know it's pancakes he wants?' Tuesday asked.

'Phht,' said Colette. 'Baxterr and I have already this morning been for a long walk in the park. You might say we are beginning to work one another out.'

'You took him for a walk?' asked Tuesday.

'Well, he joined me at 6 A.M. for my daily yoga session. And then he requested a walk

45

before the rain began. It was a beautiful dawn so we considered colours and reflections in the lake and we talked about you.'

'About me!' Tuesday exclaimed. 'What did he say?'

'He said that you, his dear friend, have lost your happiness. And that the way he misses your father is like a giant thorn in his paw.'

Tuesday lay her head on Baxterr's and hugged him. She sighed and Baxterr sighed too. She was not quite sure how she felt about her dog and her godmother talking to one another, but Baxterr licked her cheek and it was impossible for her to worry.

'There is another thing I must tell you,' Colette continued. 'I do not want you to be alarmed. Your mother is not here.'

'Not … here?'

'She has gone to the place writers go. I suspect you know this place yourself. And perhaps it is the very best place she could be right now. So, she has left me in charge.'

Tuesday frowned and nodded slowly. She was beginning to think Colette Baden-Baden was one of the most amazing people she had ever met.

'How do you know so much?' Tuesday asked, almost in a whisper.

Colette took a sip of what looked to be very strong black coffee. She made a noise through her teeth and then she said, 'Some of us had very interesting childhoods.'

This seemed to be all the answer that Colette was going to provide.

'I hope *you* weren't wanting pancakes,' she said.

Tuesday shook her head. 'They just don't taste the same since …'

'You know what?' said Colette. 'One day, when you least expect it, you will encounter the right taste again. And it will transport you. You will think that you are here, in this very kitchen, just a girl, and there he will be, your father Denis, standing by the stove, flipping pancakes and delivering them to your plate. The moment will be so warm, it will be as if the sun came from four directions at once. My guess is that it's not yet time for that. But it will be.'

'Are you sure, Colette?' Tuesday asked.

'Absolutely,' said Colette. 'But for now, boiled eggs? Some toast with marmalade?'

'Yes, please,' said Tuesday. And suddenly that was precisely what she wanted.

Chapter Six

Serendipity's journey through the night sky was strangely restful. She arrived as usual at the great tree which stood on a broad stretch of grass atop a gentle hill. But – and this was anything but usual – someone was there to meet her. It was a diminutive woman wearing a crisp mauve pants suit. She had a silken cravat at her throat and a pair of purple suede high heels on her tiny feet. Her enormous pearl earrings caught the light of a mild afternoon sun.

She was, as many of you will know, the Librarian. Holding out one of her small, wrinkled hands, she gave a meaningful cough.

At that sound, the shimmery mauve thread that had brought Serendipity on her journey coiled itself into a tidy ball that fell directly into the Librarian's palm.

'Madame Librarian,' said Serendipity. 'Is something wrong?'

'Indeed, it is,' said the Librarian. 'You have not been writing.'

Serendipity's shoulders slumped. Her head dropped. 'I haven't … I haven't been able …'

'I understand completely,' said the Librarian. 'Which is why I summoned you.'

'Summoned?'

'Yes,' said the Librarian, tossing the ball of mauve thread lightly into the air and catching it. 'When the world's most famous author suffers such a terrible loss, it is incumbent upon me to do what I can. So, here we are.'

'Yes,' said Serendipity quietly. 'But Tuesday … she …'

'Doesn't need you as much as you think. Not since her godmother arrived. Goodness, that woman took her time!' said the Librarian, her voice regaining its more usual – slightly stern – tone.

50

'But—' Serendipity began.

'I will brook no disagreement,' said the Librarian. 'Your daughter is in good – and rather large – hands. Let us walk.'

She took Serendipity's hand, threaded it through her arm and patted it. Together they set off down a path that Serendipity had followed many times in her life. It wound its way down the hill, and Serendipity was surprised how thick the fog was. She hadn't experienced such intense fog for years, not since her earliest visits.

Soon they came to the two stone lion sentinels that marked the path to the great Library. The sky, although less foggy, remained colourless, as if it couldn't quite decide what mood to be in. As they made their way up the steps and past the fountains, the mist lingered. Serendipity stared up at the single word carved on the great stone lintel above the entrance. It said IMAGINE. She sighed deeply. Imagining had been painful this past year.

'I know, dear,' the Librarian said, though Serendipity had not uttered a word. 'It will never be the same. But it will be all right. I know that's not easy to believe, but I assure you it's true.'

51

Instead of pushing open the doors to the Library, the Librarian guided Serendipity through the rose gardens and to the rear of the building, and then along a winding path Serendipity had never before seen. It led to a deep, blue lake bordered by pale grey pebbles. On the near shore, there stood a beautiful wooden boatshed. The Librarian led Serendipity to the door of the boatshed and took out of her pocket a large gold key.

'What is this place?' Serendipity asked the Librarian.

'Well,' said the Librarian. 'Writers, like everyone else, go through all the usual experiences of life. And they write about them. But sometimes, particularly if something dreadful happens, they stop writing. Cannot produce so much as a sentence. So, this is where they come.'

Serendipity frowned. 'Please don't make me write. Not yet.'

'You need not write a word. Unless you want to. Perhaps you would rather read? Some find that it's through reading that they are able to begin again. Some simply need to sleep. Rest. Draw. There's no one way.'

The Librarian pushed the door open and Serendipity stepped inside. There were bookshelves filled with books, a bed with a white counterpane, a kitchen with a table and two chairs, and a desk by the windows looking out over the balcony to the lake. Serendipity walked to the desk and ran her finger over its polished surface.

'The thing to remember is that everything you do here is right,' said the Librarian.

She opened a drawer to show Serendipity several plain notebooks, a box of pencils and several of Serendipity's favourite pens.

'The kinds of words that come at times like this are fragile. Often they cannot even stay on the page, but like to drift through the air. Sentences frequently unravel. Characters come and go as if they were, in fact, apparitions. None of that matters, as you will see. But if you allow this place to work on you …'

'But Tuesday …' Serendipity said, her eyes prickling. How could she be here when she was needed at home?

'Time is never what it seems. You know that.'

'But ...'

'Trust, Serendipity. That is your job now,' said the Librarian.

And with that she said goodbye and closed the door.

Chapter Seven

Vivienne Small woke to find she was no longer in her tree house. The room she was in was creaking, and the floor appeared to be rising and falling. Her shoulder stung from the poison dart and her head was groggy. She levered herself up and peered out the window.

'No!' she gasped. It wasn't possible. It couldn't be. But it was. She was at sea on a ship.

Shaking the tiredness from her head and limbs, Vivienne sprang towards the door and tried the handle. It wouldn't turn. She searched for an implement she could use to pick the lock. Upon a varnished writing desk were a number of brand-new quills in a glass jar. She tipped them out hurriedly and selected the sturdiest. Next, on a high shelf, she found a leather sewing pouch containing several long silver needles of the kind used for stitching sails. She drew out the thickest one, then returned to the lock. Working the quill in one direction, and the needle in the other, she listened carefully until she heard a familiar click. Carefully she eased back the lock and tested the handle. It opened!

Vivienne returned the needle to the pouch, then, considering it a rather useful find, she shoved the pouch deep inside her boot. She froze, her senses on high alert. Something was moving on the rafter above the bunk where she'd been lying. It was the merest shadow, but still she saw it.

'Ermengarde?' she whispered. 'Is that you?'

A long black nose with twitching whiskers emerged from behind a roof beam. Two dark eyes, round and shiny, observed her. Vivienne climbed onto the bunk and reached out her hand. The little rat ran down her arm and nestled on her shoulder under her hair. Vivienne tickled her under the chin.

'We may be in great danger, Ermengarde,' said Vivienne softly. 'So whatever you do, keep your wits about you.'

Ermengarde nibbled Vivienne's fingers as if to say that she understood.

'Are you ready?' Vivienne asked. 'Good.'

Easing the door open, Vivienne carefully peeked out into the corridor. It was empty. She crept along the hallway, all the while wondering how it was possible that this appeared in every way to be a cleaner, newer version of *The Silverfish*, the ship belonging to the pirate Carsten Mothwood, who had died from a fall on the Cliffs of Cartavia many moons ago. There was a silence to the ship that suggested there was nobody on board. But someone, or something, was keeping the ship on a steady course.

Vivienne sidled up the companionway, put her head out and examined the deck. She took in the clean timber decks and crisp white sails, the new ropes and polished brass. She frowned. This ship was so very similar to *The Silverfish*. But this was not that ship. Still, it was unsettling. She tiptoed out and hid behind the wheelhouse. As she did this, she had an odd memory of a girl and a dog. The vision was sudden and vivid, but just as quickly as it had come, it was gone. Peering out, she spied a tall, green creature standing at the ship's wheel. He appeared to be woven out of fresh grass. He was wearing a green shirt and shorts and he had a head of bright green hair. When he turned in her direction, she saw he had a grass-green face. She took a breath and ducked back behind the wheelhouse, but almost immediately his voice rang out.

'Ah, it's true! True and real and alive. I did capture you! And it was easy! Here you are … Vivienne Small! It's a blue day and you are on a vital *green* mission. Welcome aboard!'

Vivienne stepped out and stared at him. The grassboy left the wheel and danced his way across the deck to her in a nimble series of sideways steps. He attempted to take her hand and kiss it, but she managed to pull it away from him just in time.

The grassboy did not seem offended. 'My, you are very small, aren't you? A mere flyweight to carry! And, now that you are here, I'll be needing your writer.'

Vivienne stared at the boy. He had a shimmering quality to his eyes. They were green and gold with no dark pupils and his teeth, against his green skin, were very white. But he smelled of something that had been long underground.

'Writer?' she asked. 'What are you *talking* about? And why are we on *The Silverfish*?'

'*Silverfish*? Nonsense! This is no *Silverfish*. This is *Storm Rider*! Before you were even a thought in her head, a speck of sunlight in her eye, this was the ship she made for *me* to sail upon.'

The boy indicated the flag flying from the top of the tallest mast, and Vivienne saw that it was not emblazoned with the eye and fish skeleton she knew from *The Silverfish*, but a picture of a great wave and a jagged bolt of lightning.

'You know better than anyone, Vivienne Small, how writers can invent anything and how that changes your life! Oh yes, I'm sure you're very familiar with that!'

He said all this in a surprisingly pleasant voice, full of music, but his eyes were as cold and hard as emeralds.

'I don't understand,' said Vivienne. 'What do you mean, a writer?'

'Oh, we're so forgetful, aren't we? We have a big sleep and, oh, there they go, all those fresh and fragrant memories,' said the boy. 'C'mon, Vivienne. Snap out of it.' And he clicked his woven fingers in her face.

'Stop that,' said Vivienne, taking a step backwards.

The boy stepped forwards and clicked his fingers once more. Vivienne scowled.

But he clicked his fingers again. 'Once, twice, thrice, aren't memories nice?'

Suddenly Vivienne did remember. It almost winded her, the tumbling onrush of images of the girl Tuesday, the dog Baxterr. Tuesday and Baxterr sailing in her boat *Vivacious*. Tuesday and Baxterr in a cave making dinner. Tuesday and Baxterr swimming in a pool. Tuesday and Baxterr on a long walk with Vivienne. Tuesday being lifted into the sky in the claws of a vercaka above the City of Clocks. And Tuesday appearing through a doorway in a wall.

'There!' said the boy. 'That is your writer.

Who just happens to be *my* writer, too. Thought this was your world, didn't you? But it was mine long before you hatched from your grubby little egg.'

'Why do you need her?' asked Vivienne.

'Ah, *why*. Such an interesting question. A question alive with secrets,' said the grassboy.

'Well?' Vivienne asked.

'I'm not telling,' said the boy, shrugging. 'I'm not telling at all. Don't you know that about stories? The secrets don't come out until it's almost the end.'

Vivienne frowned.

'Secrets,' said the boy, 'are not easy to catch. Like writers.'

'Catch?' Vivienne said, swallowing.

'That's right. But today is ripe with opportunity. So summon her.'

'Summon who?'

'Your writer, you fool! Did she give you no intelligence at all?'

Vivienne was sure the boy was quite insane and that she needed to get away. She took stock of the sailing ship and considered her options.

There was no land in sight, only the wild, cold sea. But her wide blue wings could take her almost anywhere. As if reading her mind, the boy laughed and suddenly flipped himself up and spun through the air, landing on his bare green feet behind her. With lightning speed, he gripped her ankles and, in one swift movement, Vivienne found herself dangling upside down. He was strong for a boy made of grass.

She gasped, trying to wrench herself free. She felt Ermengarde's tiny claws dig into her neck. Half a second later, Ermengarde was crawling underneath the collar of Vivienne's shirt while the boy bound Vivienne's feet to the nearest boom. He bound her wrists, too, with ropes like wide lengths of paper that he had pulled from the pocket of his shorts. Vivienne strained against her bindings, but they were much too strong to break. She hung helplessly, twirling like an autumn leaf. The sewing pouch that she'd tucked in her boot tumbled onto the deck. Vivienne could see it a short distance from her nose, but the grassboy did not appear to notice it. Then she felt Ermengarde's tiny claws as the little rat climbed up her back, under her belt and continued up her leg along the inside of her trousers. Even though this was quite a tickly process, Vivienne managed to maintain her furious glare.

'So, if this ship is called *Storm Rider*, what does that make you? Prince Lightning?' Vivienne asked, keen to distract the boy while Ermengarde reached safety.

'Prince Lightning. Oh, I quite like that,' the boy said, dancing lightly around. He leaned over her and laughed. Vivienne breathed quietly, every part of her considering how she was going to escape.

'Give me a name, any name,' said the boy. 'Call me Hendrel, Phandor or Tutelaine. I have been called them all. Windish, Merivane, Irmac. I have lived the four seasons over and over. I am the Ear of Spells. I am the Eyes of Time. I am the son of Hope and the Lord of Despair. I am ...'

'Exhausting?' suggested Vivienne. She had battled many villains in her time. This particular creature was probably no worse than any of them, and there were two things she had learned from villains. The first was they wanted to be listened to. And the second was they wanted respect. So respect was the last thing Vivienne Small was going to give him.

The grass-green boy dropped to his knees and glared closely at Vivienne's upside-down face.

'Let us get to the real business at hand. Summon your writer. I am in need of her.'

'No! If you need her so badly, why don't you summon her yourself?' said Vivienne. Her head was pounding from being suspended upside down.

'I'll let you go *if* you call her for me. You see, it's been such a long time, and I want to surprise her,' said the boy in a pleading, wheedling voice.

'Cut me down, then,' said Vivienne, certain that if she only had a moment she could take flight and be gone.

Suddenly the boy noticed the sewing pouch and picked it up.

'Ah, of course,' he said. 'One stitch, two stitch, three stitch, four, I hear a writer knocking at my door.'

As he continued this rhyme, he threaded a needle.

'Five stitch, six stitch, seven and eight, I see a writer at my gate,' he said, spinning Vivienne about. Briskly, he began to stitch together the beautiful blue wings. Vivienne gritted her teeth. With each stitch the needle pierced and stung, but she refused to cry out or even whimper.

'Nine stitch, ten stitch, eleven and twelve, if you want a story you dig and delve,' continued the boy. 'Thirteen, fourteen, stitches aplenty, just six more to make it twenty.'

When he had finished, he cut her feet loose from the boom and Vivienne tumbled to the deck where she lay for a moment, winded, shocked, her wings aching and her body bruised. On the mast, not far from where Vivienne's feet had been, she spotted Ermengarde. As Vivienne watched, Ermengarde scrambled up into the safety of the rigging. *Clever girl*, Vivienne thought.

'Summon your writer,' the grassboy said, smiling. 'Come, Vivienne Small. We don't have to be enemies.'

'My wings ...' said Vivienne, through gritted teeth. She struggled to her knees.

'Tut, tut, tut, Vivienne Small. Don't you know when you're overpowered? Summon your writer.'

'You can't make me,' said Vivienne, using her bound hands to push herself upright, then scrambling to her feet.

'Oh, can't I?' he said. 'Not even if I do this?' His voice had come from Vivienne's mouth, sounding in part like himself and in part like Vivienne.

Vivienne swallowed. Had that just happened?

Then a laugh came from her throat. 'Hello, I'm Vivienne Small and a boy made of grass has gotten the better of me,' said the boy, and this time the voice was much more like Vivienne's own.

Vivienne coughed as if she might force his voice out of her throat. 'Stop it!' she said.

'Of course, dear Vivienne, I will do as you ask,' he said, though her own lips were moving against her will. 'Just summon your writer.'

'I won't,' said Vivienne, momentarily reclaiming her voice. Her eyes darted around for anything sharp she could grab to free her hands so she could fight the boy. She leapt onto the top of the wheelhouse, but she was awkward on her feet. The boy, with unexpected speed and incredible reach, swatted her and she fell once more to the deck.

'You will,' said the grassboy. 'It would have been so much better if you'd done it yourself. But no matter. He who lives alone must be resourceful.'

Out of Vivienne's mouth, in her own voice, came the boy's words, 'Writer! I summon you!'

To Vivienne's horror, a long length of greenish-silver thread appeared in front of her mouth and hovered in the air.

'No!' Vivienne cried.

'Ah, this is fun!' he said.

Again, he made Vivienne's mouth move, and her voice cried out, 'Writer! I summon you!'

More and more thread appeared as if it was drawn from an invisible and infinite supply, and in no time it was as big as a tennis ball and just out of Vivienne's reach.

'And once more for luck, I think,' the grassboy said.

Vivienne's voice rang out over the sounds of waves and creaking rigging. 'WRITER, I SUMMON YOU!'

The ball of thread instantly leapt into the air and darted high up into the sky.

'No! No! Don't come, Tuesday!' Vivienne cried, but already the thread was far, far out beyond this world and unravelling itself into another.

Chapter Eight

Tuesday and Colette spent all of that long, rainy Sunday getting to know one another. This involved several games of Cluedo and Monopoly and cribbage and pick-up-sticks and charades, as well as a frenetic card game that Colette called Spit. But when Tuesday pointed hopefully to the Scrabble set, Colette scowled.

'With a writer? You have to be joking,' she said.

It was a day that was slow and fast all at once, and when evening came, Tuesday found that she was still in the pyjama pants, T-shirt and hooded top that she'd been wearing at breakfast. Her clothes bore some marks from the sausages and mash she and Colette had whipped up for a late lunch – Colette having made a quick trip out for supplies, and finding in the pantry things that Tuesday had long overlooked.

'How about we do some unpacking?' suggested Colette. 'Work up an appetite before dinner? Hmm?'

The majority of Colette's many silver cases had been stowed behind the couch in the living room since she had arrived. What they contained, Tuesday now discovered, was all manner of camera equipment and film footage. By taking down a few paintings, Colette turned one wall of the room into a screen, and showed Tuesday some of her work-in-progress. The first sequence opened with a picture of a tiny child with a star-shaped tattoo on its forehead, sleeping against the flanks of an enormous white-furred animal that Tuesday was fairly sure was a reindeer. The camera pulled back to show purple mountains and meadows dotted with yellow flowers, and people dressed in layers and layers of colourful clothes. Then, in a heartbeat, the same child was a young boy weaving through a grazing herd of reindeer, appearing and disappearing between and behind the animals' stocky legs. And then he was older again, longer haired and serious, sitting astride a reindeer with a strand of grass between his teeth. He and the reindeer reached the edge of a milky, aqua stream that coursed through dark rocks, and the animal bent to drink.

'It's like another world,' Tuesday said softly.

'There are worlds within the world. That is one thing I have learned from all my travels,' Colette said. She nodded towards the screen and said, 'Here, now, is another.'

This sequence began with the huge liquid eyes of a tiny girl strapped to her mother's back with a length of saffron-yellow cloth. The mother was poling a small boat down a flat, brown river. The child's limbs were bare and Tuesday could almost feel the humidity of the jungle that pushed in towards the water on both sides. Then the same girl was singing as she sat at a rough table on a jetty on the riverbank, and although she couldn't have been more than five, she was expertly flicking the scales from the sides of a large, weed-coloured fish. The scene changed and the girl effortlessly transformed into a young woman standing on the same jetty, a huge red flower braided into her hair. She was talking to a man in a boat, her face calm and determined as she named her price for the fish in the bucket beside her.

'You've seen such incredible things. These places you've been, the people you've seen ... they're amazing,' Tuesday said, with a sigh that was almost sad.

Colette observed Tuesday intensely. Tuesday, in turn, observed the lines that framed Colette's mouth and fanned out from the corners of her eyes. In the light from the film her hazel eyes looked green, but at other times – Tuesday had noticed – those same eyes looked brown, and at other times they appeared flecked with gold.

'You will remember, Tuesday. You will,' Colette said.

'Remember what?'

'That every day has the possibility of a little magic,' her godmother said.

Tuesday smiled wistfully.

'It is a hard thing,' said Colette, tapping the side of her head, 'to remember and never forget. We are always forgetting things, losing them in our brains. Store something in the wrong drawer inside your head, and lo, it is forgotten!'

Tuesday nodded. One of the things she was most afraid of was that she would forget her father – that time would gradually erase him. It panicked her the way time had refused to stop when he died, even though it felt as if it should have done. It didn't seem right that the sun had kept rising and setting, that days kept beginning and ending, each new one carrying her just a little further from the last time she had spoken with him, hugged him, seen his face.

'Come on, kiddo,' said Colette. 'We have watched enough pictures. Why don't you check if your mother is back yet? Maybe she will eat dinner with us.'

Tuesday managed to rekindle something of her smile. 'Okay,' she said.

'C'mon, doggo,' said Colette to Baxterr, who was snoozing on the rug. 'Let's see what we can make in the kitchen.'

Tuesday took most of the stairs two at a time, but slowed as she approached the last flight, the one that led to her mother's writing room. Tuesday had hardly been in this room since her father had died.

Standing at the threshold, Tuesday remembered vividly the first time she had ever used her mother's typewriter, and how she had first discovered the silver thread that had the power to take a writer *there*. She would never forget how it felt to be transported to the tree on the hill, to visit the great Library with the Librarian, or to meet Vivienne Small. But all those things seemed so distant and long ago that it was almost as if they belonged to another Tuesday McGillycuddy.

Tuesday switched on the light. It was clear Serendipity had not returned. In the centre of the room was Colette's hammock and, piled in it, was Colette's coat. At its tips, the black fur felt coarse, almost like Tuesday imagined a yak might feel if you were patting one. But further in, the fur was rich and plush. It smelled of pine needles and wood smoke. She made a mental note to ask Colette how she had come by it.

Beside the coat was a rolled blanket striped in colours that made Tuesday think of a carnival in the desert: gold and aqua, rose and yellow. She opened it out, then she realised it wasn't a blanket at all, but a poncho. She thought that Colette wouldn't mind if she tried it on. It came down over her hands and the bottom almost touched her feet. It was warm and soft, and she hugged it to herself. It too smelled of pine trees and wood smoke, and she thought that Colette was possibly the most interesting godmother anyone ever had.

Tuesday whirled about, watching the poncho's colours blur. When she steadied herself, she was facing Serendipity's desk. Right in the middle of it was her mother's beautiful typewriter, still threaded with the blank and abandoned page. Tuesday felt a draught from the window, which had been left ever so slightly ajar. She lay a hand on the glass. Rain was melting the city lights beyond the pane and everything was shimmering. And then, with a shock, Tuesday realised that there was a thread outside the window. As she watched, it tapped urgently on the glass. Then it snaked through the narrow gap between the window and the sill and slithered into the room, swerving from side to side as if searching for something.

Tuesday reached out her hand. The thread was green. *How unusual*, she thought. The thread seemed to suddenly sense her presence. It turned and darted at her hand, wrapping itself quickly around her wrist.

'Oh!' she said. 'Hello. What a very insistent thread you are. And you're green. I've never seen a green thread bef— Ouch!'

The thread tightened around her wrist so hard that it felt as if it might cut into her skin.

'You're hurting!' Tuesday said, and she tried to peel the thread off.

It wouldn't budge. It made Tuesday afraid.

'Baxterr,' Tuesday called. And then, louder, 'Doggo? Baxterr! Colette?'

Downstairs, Baxterr's ears pricked and he launched himself out of the kitchen and up the stairs. But by the time he had run the five flights to Serendipity's writing room, the window was wide open, and Tuesday was nowhere to be seen.

He was a small and ordinary dog when he leapt up onto the desk and peered anxiously out the window. But then a miraculous transformation began. Baxterr grew wings. They spread from him with as little effort as it takes for you to spread your hands. They were golden brown and furry, just like the rest of him. He was growing, too. He was no longer a small dog, but a decidedly large dog.

And then, just as Baxterr was about to take flight through the window, there came a voice from behind him.

'My, look at you! *Magnifique! Wunderbar!* But I hope you're not dashing off without telling me where you're going!' said Colette Baden-Baden.

Baxterr whined, his gaze not moving from the darkness outside.

'Well, maybe she doesn't need you on this occasion,' suggested Colette.

Baxterr barked.

'I see,' said Colette. 'And you are quite sure there's something wrong?'

Baxterr barked again, a little more gently this time.

'Very well. I understand. But I shall need to accompany you.'

'Hurrrrrr,' said Baxterr.

'You are forgetting that I also made a promise to Serendipity that I would take care of Tuesday. Just as you are a dog of your word, I am a woman of my mine.'

Baxterr whined and cocked his head.

'I do not care if it is irregular. I know you would do an excellent job of protecting Tuesday from whatever you think may have befallen her, but you are not going alone. Whether you like it or not, I was put in charge.'

Baxterr turned his head, then glided to the floor beside Colette.

'Well,' she said. 'You have to be more comfortable than a camel. Just let me get my coat and hat.'

And so it was that if, for a moment, you had glanced up on that rainy night a few minutes later, you might – if you were lucky – have caught sight of the silhouette of what appeared to be a bear riding a colossal bird. The bear was, of course, Colette Baden-Baden in her fur coat and hat, and the bird, of course, was Baxterr. Behind them the lights were still on at Brown Street, but nobody was home.

Chapter Nine

Tuesday's flight across the sky was no gentle or meandering journey. The green thread had yanked her out of the window and up into rain so fast she'd hardly had time to catch her breath. Never had she known a thread to pull so hard. She squinted into the rain. It stung her eyes and chilled her hands. She pulled Colette's poncho tight about her, grateful for its size and warmth.

She wondered what was so urgent that she had been hauled off like this. Did her mother need her? Or was it Vivienne? And where was Baxterr? Tuesday peered back through the falling rain, sure her dog would be flying after her.

'Baxterr!' she called. '*Baxterr!*'

But he was nowhere to be seen.

Then, abruptly, the rain stopped. The clouds, the city and the weather disappeared. Below, above and all around her, Tuesday could see nothing but stars. She was still hurtling behind the green string that was attached firmly – too firmly – to her outstretched arm and about her waist.

And so they went on, Tuesday and the thread, through the darkness, going at such a speed that her hair began to dry out. She wriggled her toes. *No shoes.* She was wearing the socks she had left the house in, and they were still damp with rain.

At last she could see a familiar distant point of light ahead, and a little of the worry that had accompanied her since being pulled so ruthlessly through the window, started to melt away. Soon Tuesday could see the mounded peak of a green hill with a single, ancient tree.

'There'd better be a good reason for this,' she muttered into the rushing air.

She looked behind her again, searching the sky for any sign of Baxterr, but there was none.

She had never been here without him, and it didn't feel right.

She braced for landing as the thread swooped down towards the tree, but the thread did not let go.

'Wait!' Tuesday yelled, struggling against the string. 'Wait!'

The string swept her around the tree, but still it did not let her go.

'I don't mean to be rude,' Tuesday called to the tree, 'but I need shoes! Whatever you think might work! I'm sorry, but I seem to be in a hurry!'

The thread pulled Tuesday up and away from the tree, and she thought perhaps the tree might not have heard her. But suddenly two items came flying through the sky as if catapulted from the tree's highest branches. The first one she caught firmly. The second one zoomed to the left of her, and she lunged for it. They were shoes: rainbow-coloured runners with green laces. Inside one of them was a dry pair of socks.

'Thank you,' she called back to the tree, and although its leaves gave a brief shiver, Tuesday was already too far away to see.

On and on she was pulled, over acres and acres of mist, then without warning the thread swerved downwards. Tuesday was plunged into whiteness, then she dropped out of the mist into a dark wintry sky. A blast of salty, ice-whipped wind rushed into her face as she picked up speed once again. Tuesday grasped the shoes firmly against her as she skimmed over a stormy sea. Huge waves crashed against towering rocky outcrops. Recognising the contours of the cliffs and bays, Tuesday saw it was the Restless Sea, and she felt a thrill of relief. But the weather was far wilder than she had ever known it to be in the world of Vivienne Small, and the air was bitterly cold. She stared down at the land and saw that it was white with snow and ice and the Peppermint Forest was steel grey.

In the distance, further out to sea, rising and falling on mountains of white-veined water, was a ship. Tuesday knew the vicious, sharp lines of its hull, but the vessel appeared to have been freshly painted in gleaming black, and its white sails looked new. There was no sign of the mould stains and ragged seams she knew so well. Speeding behind the thread, Tuesday gained on the ship, and was soon close enough to see that although the sails were trimmed for the weather, and the ship was making its way steadily windwards, there were no sailors in the rigging. Only one figure stood at the wheel. Tuesday saw a flash of green, brilliant as her thread, and then realised there was a second person by the wheelhouse. A very small person.

Suddenly Tuesday was coming in to land on the ship's deck unpleasantly fast. She had enough time to make out Vivienne Small standing beside a tall green creature with wild and vivid hair, before she was dropped unceremoniously on the hard, slippery deck. The thread unravelled and rolled itself into a ball, then disappeared as if it was a candle flame that had been snuffed out.

Tuesday, rubbing her knee where it had hit the deck, scrambled up to greet Vivienne. But the green person loomed over her, grinning as if he had never been more pleased to see anyone in his life, and one of his arms was wrapped menacingly around Vivienne's neck.

What a bizarre creature, Tuesday thought. He appeared to be a boy tightly woven from long, stretchy strands of grass. Vivienne was tiny beside him and her face was more angular, as if the bones of her cheeks and jaw were a little more defined. Thin, thought Tuesday. And then Tuesday noticed Vivienne's wings. Still leathery, still blue, but large enough to take Vivienne anywhere. Tuesday couldn't help but feel a thrill of wonder at seeing them, until she realised that the beautiful blue wings were sewn together crudely at their edges with what looked like fishing line. Had the boy done this to her?

'It wasn't me that called. It wa—' Vivienne croaked, but the grassboy only tightened his grip on her throat.

'Do hush, Vivienne Small,' he said, squeezing a pained sound out of her. 'We have a guest, and my, isn't the day suddenly *green* with promise?'

'What have you done to her? Let her go!' Tuesday said, leaping at the grassboy and trying to wrestle his arm away from Vivienne. She was surprised how sinewy his arm felt, and how effortlessly he slipped from her grip, sliding Vivienne away with him.

'Writer! Aren't you pleased to see me? Where

is my greeting? Where are your tears of joy at seeing me again? Aren't you glad I didn't die in the breaking day?'

Tuesday frowned. 'Who are you?'

'Don't you dare pretend you don't remember,' he said.

'I don't know what you mean,' said Tuesday.

He squeezed his arm against Vivienne's neck again and she winced, but her eyes were fierce and Tuesday was in no doubt that she and Vivienne had to find a way to distract this creature. He seemed to think Tuesday knew him. But she didn't. She had never seen him before in her life.

'I'm sorry,' Tuesday said. 'It was such an unexpected journey, terribly fast, and I'm not thinking straight. My feet are wet, you see, and I never think straight when my feet are wet.' With this, Tuesday indicated her damp socks. 'Would you help me peel them off? It's freezing and I swear my fingers and toes are turning blue.'

The boy blinked.

'Please?' said Tuesday.

'I'll help,' said Vivienne, her voice squeezed by the boy's arm.

86

'Very well,' said the boy, releasing Vivienne and pushing her roughly towards Tuesday.

'Run!' said Tuesday, the moment Vivienne was free. Then she kicked at the boy's knee in an attempt to stop him running after Vivienne. But just at that moment a huge wave hit the ship. Tuesday and Vivienne were flung into the air before falling heavily to the deck. Vivienne, with her hands and wings tied, landed on her stomach. Tuesday banged her elbow hard on the wooden floor, one shoe sliding out of her grasp. The boy did a perfect mid-air cartwheel and landed with one foot on Vivienne's back. He laughed, entirely unperturbed by the violent motion of the ship.

'Neither of you is going anywhere, is that clear?' he said. 'At least not until I say so. Now, Writer, do please tell me that you remember me.'

Tuesday frowned, and then she simply shook her head.

The boy screamed. It was an anguished cry of rage and frustration.

'How dare you?' he said. 'I saved you. *You're my only friend*, that's what you used to say. You promised me you'd never forget me. Then you left me down there.'

Tuesday glanced at Vivienne, who was struggling to get to her feet. But the boy's foot kept her pinned to the deck.

'It's been a long time, hasn't it, Writer? But we're together again now,' he added in a sing-song voice.

Tuesday inched over and retrieved the shoe that had been flung away. She began peeling off her damp socks and replacing them with the dry ones. Then she put on the new shoes and laced them up. She did all of this slowly and gently, trying not to hold the attention of the green boy without angering him further. If she had another chance to escape she wanted to be ready. The boy kept talking.

'I waited,' he said. 'You promised: *I'll always tell you stories. I'll send them every day.* But you stopped. I waited. I did busy things. But it wasn't enough. I got hungrier and hungrier, but you didn't send stories. And then the breaking day came. Everything went wobbly like the earth had become the sea. I thought it was the end of the world. I dug and I dug. I brought *Storm Rider* with me. Look how big she grew! Look how big I grew! Then I found this world. And I found *her*.' He stared down at Vivienne Small.

Tuesday frowned. A ship called *Storm Rider*? It was strikingly similar to *The Silverfish*, as if this was *The Silverfish*, new and sparkling. But the boy was still talking.

'I thought if you wouldn't come for me, you were sure to come for *her*. All those stories you sent me about *her*. So I found Vivienne Small. And now she has done her job.'

He hauled Vivienne up and put her back on her feet. Vivienne stared at Tuesday meaningfully. Then, with a flick of her eyes, she glanced up into the rigging above them. Tuesday gave Vivienne a tiny nod of understanding, but didn't dare follow her gaze.

The boy leaned down and smiled at the scowling Vivienne. His voice was sweet as he said, 'Oh dear, small Vivienne Small, it's time for you to leave this story. Any last words? Well, then, goodbye.'

With that, he lifted Vivienne by one arm,

and with enormous strength, swung her up into the air and flung her over the side of the ship. Vivienne flew through the air then plummeted into the roiling sea, her feet, her body, her head and then her blue wingtips disappearing into the trough of a wave.

'No!' Tuesday screamed.

But the boy only laughed. 'You can't have both of us. It would never work!'

Tuesday raced to the side of the ship and searched the sea for any sign of Vivienne surfacing. But the waves were high and steep. She thought she saw a flash of leathery blue there, or maybe over there? But the ship sailed swiftly on, away, away, from what might have been Tuesday's last glimpse of Vivienne Small.

'How dare you!' Tuesday said, momentarily forgetting the power the boy could wield and flinging herself at him. 'You've killed her! You've killed Vivienne Small!'

'Dear me,' said the boy, chuckling and again slipping from her grip with uncanny speed and agility. 'You aren't listening, Writer! This is my story. There's no place for Vivienne Small or anyone else I don't choose. It's going to be just like old times.'

Tuesday was beginning to feel quite sick. Maybe it was the speed of her flight from Brown Street, or the truly shocking things she had observed since she arrived, or possibly just the swell of the ocean beneath the ship, but suddenly she thought she might vomit.

'My, you've turned a wonderful shade of green,' the boy said, appearing quite delighted.

'I don't understand,' said Tuesday, lurching for the railing. She took a deep breath as she did her best to quell her stomach. But it was no good. It might have been a long time since lunch with Colette, and she'd had no chance to eat dinner at all, but still she vomited over the side of the ship until she could vomit no more.

At last, she turned around and stared at the boy, who had clearly been waiting for her.

'Who are you?' she asked.

'I'm Loddon,' said the boy, perplexed, laughing. 'Loddon! You must remember me. You gave me my box to keep me safe.'

Something shifted inside Tuesday. A little drawer in her memory sprang open and she heard her mother telling her a rhyme.

At the bottom of the garden, underneath the tree,
The boy called Loddon calls to me.

Tuesday couldn't remember what came next. But she remembered how it ended.

Perhaps he still calls, I don't know,
I put him in a box far down below.

'Loddon?' she murmured.

No, it couldn't be. He was just an imaginary boy in a poem – a boy Serendipity had told her about, the one who was always hungry for stories. But what was he doing here? And why had he called her?

'Yes!' said Loddon, holding his hands together and smiling at her. 'That's right. And we're together again. At last.'

Chapter Ten

Over the course of her life, Colette Baden-Baden had done many remarkable things. She had explored sweltering jungles, climbed blue glaciers, crossed tangerine deserts, traversed rainbow-coloured sandstone cliffs and ascended goat tracks to pinnacles above the clouds. But this was her first time aboard a flying dog and her heart was hurtling at full gallop as Baxterr soared into the night sky.

Unlike many people, who close their eyes when they're frightened, Colette had the unusual affliction, when terrified, of being unable to blink. Her eyes were pinned wide as saucers as the city below, with its tall buildings and wide streets and leafy parks and glittering carpet of lights, gradually receded to a distant glow. At last Colette's ears popped and somehow that made her eyelids blink, and when she opened them again, the city was gone and there was only the reassuring, rhythmic beating of Baxterr's furry wings transporting them through a star-sprinkled blanket of sky. It was then that Colette realised how tightly her hands were holding two fistfuls of fur at the back of Baxterr's neck.

'Well, doggo,' said Colette at last, 'you are remarkable. This flying … it is exhilarating. I like it.'

'Ruff,' Baxterr responded.

At that moment, a hint of light appeared on the horizon – a golden haze of the kind that you sometimes see out the window of an aeroplane when you are flying towards a new day faster than it can possibly run away. Just as writers rarely venture anywhere without a pencil and notepad, Colette rarely went anywhere without a camera. As she took in the remarkable sight before her, she cursed herself for only grabbing her coat and hat in her haste, and not running back downstairs to grab her equipment. She doubted anyone had ever filmed the place she was heading towards and certainly not from the back of a Winged Dog. And at that thought she again felt the thrill of amazement that here she was, on a flying dog, going who knew where, and that thrill went all the way up her spine.

The gold rim of light grew larger and larger, until the sky brightened to a soft blue above a dense ellipse of cloud. Peeping out of the cloud was a green hillside, and on the hillside was a single, magnificent tree. It was as wide as the widest boab Colette had ever seen, and Baxterr was making directly for it. Above the tree, he banked in a steep arc, causing Colette to slip sideways and grasp Baxterr's fur even more tightly.

'Was that quite necessary?' Colette asked.

'Ruff,' said Baxterr.

'Not fun exactly,' said Colette. 'A little advance warning might be—'

Baxterr barked.

Colette said, 'Okay, but why?'

Before Colette received an explanation, Baxterr plunged right through the cloud that rimmed the hillside. Mist swirled around Colette's face before they emerged not into a sunlit world, as she had expected, but again into a darkness that might have been night, only bigger than any night she had known. The darkness was teeming with globes, and other shapes. They were red and stripy, or orange and yellow with spots. They were ruby and emerald, sapphire and turquoise, opal and tourmaline. They were spherical and oblong, in the shape of obelisks and crescents, jellyfish and starfish, spirals and helices. It was as if she were under the sea, and yet she was not under the sea. The floating things were huge, they were tiny, they were racing around and slowly drifting. They were transparent or opaque, patterned, glittering, shimmering like moonlight in water or as black as a cat at midnight. Colette's eyes did not blink, and her jaw fell open, and she turned her head this way and that doing her best to take in this extraordinary and unimaginable sight. Where were they? Had she fallen out of the universe she knew and into another? Yes, she considered. Yes, she almost certainly had.

Baxterr flew with clear intent. His nose was pointed towards one particular sphere, a huge globe with a faint rainbow shimmer as if it were reflecting sunlight through rain. As they flew closer, Colette could see, through the rainbow glow, a mountain range sheathed in snow, and further away tracts of deep forest. She could see a bitter wind-whipped sea and tall, forbidding cliffs. Could it be? Why of course, she thought. She might have been far from Brown Street for ten years, but the wonder of travel was there were always places to find books – new or second-hand – and Colette was as familiar with the world of Vivienne Small as you are.

They are all worlds, she thought, gazing about her. *They are the worlds of writers.* This was such an extraordinary revelation that her eyes watered and a single tear ran down her cheek.

'Ruff, ruff,' Baxterr instructed as he put back his ears and folded his wings.

Colette braced, realising that they were about to pierce the glassy membrane and enter the world of Vivienne Small. Baxterr, of course, passed effortlessly through this shimmering exterior – nose, eyes, ears, shoulders. But the same was not true of Colette Baden-Baden. She smacked into the membrane like an insect against the windscreen of a car. She lost hold of Baxterr's fur and tried desperately to cling on, but the glassy surface was as slippery as a soap bubble. Baxterr continued on, and Colette began to slide and then, as there was nothing to hold on to, she began to fall.

Colette fell and fell, and her heart flew up into her throat as if a small bird were lodged there, flapping wildly in terror. *If it is in my throat, then it must be a swallow*, Colette thought to herself, and the joke reminded her to laugh, for it had always been a plan of hers to meet death with a smile on her face.

Down through the sky she tumbled, head over feet, head over feet. The worlds around her whirled and glowed, baubles of colour and phosphorescence. She thought that this must be what it would be like to be an ant floating inside a kaleidoscope.

'So, Colette, you are going to die,' she said to herself matter-of-factly as she fell. 'It is not such a terrible way to go, falling from a flying dog. I am seeing incredible things. I am seeing the worlds of writers. This is not something dying people see every day.'

Indeed Colette was seeing incredible things in the worlds she was falling past. Was that a waterfall of chocolate? Was that a green sheep? Was that a bear walking beside a boy who was riding a wolf? Was that a girl in a red sequinned suit atop a high-wire? Was that a submarine under the sea?

Colette continued to talk to herself as she fell. 'You remember what you learned at skydiving school. Nothing hurts except the landing. And even that probably not for more than the briefest moment. There may not be time to feel any pain at all. It might all just go black. Or yellow. Or green. I would like it to go orange. A bright, edible orange. It's a better death than starving. Better than drowning, too. *Much* better than burning. Yes, falling will do. Falling is not so bad.'

Colette began to feel a little light-headed, as if she were high in the mountains where oxygen was a luxury.

'There is a problem though, Colette, is there not? If you die, you will break your promise to care for Tuesday until Serendipity returns. So I think you cannot die. Not yet. Not even in this pleasant falling-through-worlds kind of way. You must try to stop falling.'

But of course, as some of you may yet discover, attempting to defy gravity is not an easy thing to do. It takes lift and thrust, feathered or reptilian wings, or some sophisticated engineering. None of which was immediately available to Colette. And so it was that after a little while, the worlds became blurrier, her thoughts became more distant, and her eyes closed. Despite her best efforts to maintain consciousness (which included an attempt to sing opera), Colette Baden-Baden passed out.

Chapter Eleven

Some time after passing out, Colette Baden-Baden fell onto a large ottoman. It was covered in brown and white cowhide that matched a nearby chair, two rugs and a pair of couches that were set around a glowing fire. In its final moments, her landing was more of a gentle descent than a plummet, and when her body met with the ottoman, it simply behaved like good custard. It spread. Stomach down, head to one side, arms and legs splayed out, Colette sprawled. She did not immediately wake up, which meant that the man sitting a short distance away at a desk of instruments – who had been intently working on the insides of something that resembled a large fishbowl – had plenty of time to consider the fallen creature, and then walk across the large room to observe it more closely.

The man, as some of you may have guessed, was the Gardener. He noticed that the furry creature on his ottoman was snoring gently. He peered at it and saw that despite the bearskin coat, beaver-skin boots and racoon hat (he knew his wild animals), this was in fact a woman. The Gardener scratched a white scraggly beard and gazed up into the open roof above his rooms in the Conservatory.

'Once upon a time,' he said, 'I'd have done most anything to have a woman fall from the sky. But now it's happened, I'm not at all sure what to do about it.'

He looked down at himself. The shirt he was wearing was the same one he'd been wearing both day and night for a length of time that might have been weeks. There was evidence of several meals and splashes of black coffee on both shirt and trousers. Under the nails of his hands, and embedded into the knuckles, was earth and sand, mud and grit, glue and paint. His hair hung down his back in a braid that resembled a frayed and ancient rope. His boots were dusty and he suspected he smelled like the camping swag he liked to take with him when he journeyed out to inspect the worlds beyond the Conservatory.

'Perhaps it's time for some personal grooming,' he said to himself, still observing the woman.

Since becoming the Gardener, he had been perplexed by managing any sort of a schedule. Worlds needed routine maintenance, and they had their own unique rhythms that had nothing to do with anything he could organise. He had discovered that he simply couldn't predict when a writer was going to cause upheaval. If he couldn't solve a problem from the Conservatory – using the instruments and implements that were arrayed on shelves and in drawers and boxes – he would need to go in to the world and inspect it. Sometimes this took days and weeks, and there was always a backlog.

If it was a simple task, like stopping a river from bursting through a dam, or ensuring a certain species didn't get out of control and kill everything else, or cleaning up after a severe storm, then the Gardener could do all he needed to do from the comfort of the Conservatory. However, other things were more complicated. A newly created world sometimes needed help maintaining a steady axis, or grew so fast it endangered itself and others. Old worlds became fragile and threatened to drift away altogether, and he had to lasso them back. Occasionally, a whole host of minor characters would end up floating in the middle of vast oceans or stranded on the wrong side of a disaster area. It fell to the Gardener to rescue or reroute, and these were no easy tasks.

In the Conservatory there were no days or nights. No weeks or months either, technically. The sun did not rise. The sun did not set. The Gardener simply lived amid the perpetual swirl of worlds in infinite darkness. Whenever he thought it must be breakfast time, breakfast food appeared on the long side table. It was the same with dinner. But he'd had several spells, since he'd taken over from the previous Gardener, when he ate nothing but breakfast for every meal. Apart from his dog, Apache, who was curled up asleep on the rug, he did not have company at all. But now company had arrived, in the form of a furry woman, and he thought he'd best be hospitable.

So when Colette Baden-Baden awoke, the first thing she saw was a pair of fancy snakeskin cowboy boots polished to a high gleam, a pair of long legs in faded yet neatly pressed jeans, a belt buckle with a buffalo skull, a shirt in red check with pearl buttons and, above all that, the clean-shaven face of a man with a fine head of white hair, neatly tied back, and a pair of warm blue eyes, observing her from a couch close by.

'Good afternoon,' he said. 'I am the Gardener and I made coffee.' He spoke with a particular twang.

He poured Colette a cup from a pot on a table beside him as she sat up and took in the extra-ordinary room. She observed the cowhide rugs and portraits of painted ponies prancing across wide-open prairies. Two identical hatstands were hung with a collection of cowboy hats, every one of them white, though some were grubbier and older than others. Along one wall, from a row of metal hooks, hung coils of rope in various thicknesses and lengths. There was also a boathook leaning against the same wall. A cheerful fire blazed in a circular fireplace in front of which, regarding her with curiosity, lay an enormous white dog with a deep brown patch over one eye.

'I think you might have saved my life,' said Colette to the man, wondering if in fact she was dead, and this was some of kind afterlife. He handed her a cup and Colette breathed in the scent of hickory. She was very partial to hickory.

'Are you a writer?' Colette frowned.

'Oh, I was. But now I'm the Gardener. Nice to meet you, ma'am.'

'Colette Baden-Baden,' said Colette gruffly, shaking the Gardener's outstretched hand, still uncertain what to make of all this.

'Well, Ms Baden-Baden,' said the Gardener, in his long drawl, 'you seem a little unstuck from whatever was your purpose before you landed here. Where exactly were you going, or what had been your intention when you set out? My experience, limited though it is, would indicate that it's mighty unusual for people to just drop in.'

Colette took a deep breath. The coffee was

beginning to make her feel a little more solid. She still wasn't sure she was alive, but it appeared that she wasn't dead. She wasn't sure if this Gardener was of sound mind, but he was probably no madder than many people she had met. She pursed her lips and began to organise an answer to this most difficult question. She considered what she could say to this man about Serendipity and Tuesday, Brown Street and threads, and the fact she had come on a flying dog. But before she could open her mouth, Baxterr flew in and landed on the broad rug.

'Ha!' grunted Colette. 'So you found me!'

'Ruff,' said Baxterr, resuming his everyday size and wingless shape, which made him look like an innocently small, shaggy, golden, brown-eyed dog. He bounded up to Colette.

'Ruff, ruff, ruff,' he continued. This was accompanied by a great deal of tail wagging, eye contact and pawing of her knees.

'Oh, you don't say,' said Colette. 'Well, it wasn't exactly pleasant for me either. I know you warned me, but until it happened I didn't under-stand why a person who was not a writer ...'

'Baxterr?' said the Gardener.

'Ruff,' said Baxterr, spinning around to regard the Gardener. 'Ruff, ruff, ruff!'

'Rooof,' said the enormous dog, standing up and wagging her tail. She completely dwarfed Baxterr, and when she nosed him playfully with her strong muzzle, she knocked him right off his feet. Baxterr righted himself, as if nothing untoward had happened at all, and returned to his conversation with Colette.

'Ruff, ruff, ruff,' he said.

'Yes, I know you are bursting at the seams to find Tuesday, and so am I. But maybe this is a good place to get help, yes?' said Colette.

The big white dog gave another deep, friendly 'Rooof', wagged her tail, and regarded Baxterr questioningly.

Colette said, 'I think I can answer your query. He wants to leave, even though he's just arrived, because he's worried about his human.'

'Of course. Young Tuesday,' the Gardener said, with a frown. 'But how did she and Baxterr get separated? I'm sure that's not regular.'

'Ruff,' confirmed Baxterr.

The Gardener turned to Colette. 'Let me introduce myself again. I am the Gardener, but my name is Silver Nightly, and let me say that any friend of Baxterr or Tuesday is a true friend of mine.'

'Ruff, ruff,' said Baxterr.

'Rooof, rooof,' said Silver Nightly's dog.

Colette sighed. 'Where to begin?' she murmured, before sharing with Silver Nightly the news about Denis, and describing the terrible year that had followed his death. And then, without mentioning names or specifics, she told him how Tuesday's mother had gone away and how she, Colette, as Tuesday's godmother, had made a solemn promise to take care of Tuesday for the duration of her mother's absence.

'As you can see,' said Colette. 'We are in need of quite urgent help. It seems I cannot get to the world of Vivienne Small to find Tuesday because the laws of this universe simply do not allow it. I am not a writer. But Baxterr, it appears, can go anywhere. And your dog, Apache, is the same?'

'You know her name?' asked Silver Nightly.

'She told me herself,' said Colette.

109

Silver Nightly was startled.

'She decided, no doubt, that I am a person who can be trusted with a name. But please, what do you suggest for our predicament?'

Silver Nightly ran a hand through his white hair. 'Well, you're an anomaly, Ms Baden–Baden. I think there's only one person who might be able to solve this. And that is the Librarian.'

'The Librarian?'

'Yup. She's a mighty interesting woman. Not a good one to cross. But, in a fix like this, given Tuesday's age, I know she'd want to be sure that young lady was safely in her story and getting along with it. I don't think for a moment she'll let you intervene. But I don't suppose it can hurt to ask.'

'And where is this Librarian?' asked Colette, observing the two jetties that stretched away from the room as if they might be expecting a ship to sail in at any moment. She also observed how only one jetty had a door leading to it.

'Oh, no,' laughed Silver Nightly. 'Madame Librarian is in the great Library. It's about as far from here as it's possible to get. You might say if this is the South Pole, then she's at the North. But she has a way of knowing everything. When I made a few errors in my early time here, overdid my job a little, stopped an invasion, found a letter, got a boy reunited with the girl he loved, she had some harsh things to say. It's a delicate thing. A little intervention can cause a lot of chaos. Gardening is a … well … a vocation.'

'Can you show me a little of your work?' Colette asked.

Baxterr whined and cocked his head.

'I may never come this way again, doggo. A few minutes and we'll be on our way. How I wish I had brought my camera.'

Baxterr seemed to accept this, though his tail quivered and his paws were restless. Anyone who knew him well would understand he was feeling impatient, but trying to be polite and not show it.

Silver Nightly walked with Colette to a long bench with an array of instruments and metal arms each holding a spherical object covered with a cloth. He took the cover from one of these spheres and handed Colette a peculiar pair of spectacles that were like the glasses optometrists use to examine your eyes.

'If you use these, you'll be able to see a whole lot better,' he said.

Colette slid on the spectacles and peered into the world that was now greatly magnified. She could see a city. The old stone buildings stood proud and tall, and in the streets a crowd had gathered. Some people carried torches, others carried red flags, and all were marching and possibly singing. Colette observed the black glint of cannons being manoeuvred over cobblestones. And in front of them was a great stone building she was sure was the Bastille, the famous French prison. But all of it was frozen, as if a magic wand had been waved and stopped them all in their tracks.

'The fourteenth of July, 1789,' she whispered.

Silver Nightly chuckled. 'You have no idea how often I've had to remake those flags! They get terribly torn up.'

'But they don't notice that everything stops, the people there?'

'I think it's as if they all blinked in unison,' said Silver Nightly.

Suddenly Colette had a sense of something looming above her. When she looked up, still wearing the Gardener's spectacles, she saw a gigantic world, apparently about to squash them. She let out an alarmed noise before Silver Nightly had the presence of mind to whip the glasses off her face, and Colette could see that although a world *was* coming in close to the Conservatory, it was still a good way off.

'Oh, that's mighty interesting. Mighty interesting' said Silver Nightly, rubbing his chin.

'What is it doing?' Colette asked.

'Oh, it's coming in for routine maintenance,' Silver said. 'Truth is, I've had it on my priority list. It's been worrying me. But still, the timing is remarkably apt.'

Colette watched in amazement as the world approached one of the long piers leading out from the side of the Conservatory. There it landed and rolled towards them along the pier, growing smaller as it came closer until at last, when it slid through a hatch in the wall of the Conservatory, it was the size of a large fishbowl. It came to land, by way of a glass chute, on a velvet cushion on the Gardener's bench with a quiet *hsssssssss* sound.

Baxterr got up off the floor from beside Apache and trotted over to the workbench.

'Ruff, ruff,' he said, and sniffed close to the world.

'Smart dog,' Silver Nightly said. 'That there is none other than the world of Vivienne Small.'

Colette remembered the highly polished exterior of the world that she had only recently slid off.

'This might save us all a lot of trouble,' she said, watching as Silver Nightly swung a hinged lamp over the world and removed a section of its exterior as if it were a lid.

Silver Nightly hesitated. 'By rights, I shouldn't let you get involved. But since you're as good as family, and she is so very young, I'll let you take a peek.'

Colette sat down in Silver Nightly's work chair and repositioned the spectacles. She stared into the world of Vivienne Small. There was the Restless Sea, and the snow-covered Mountains of Margalov. There was the Peppermint Forest, deep in winter. There was the River of Rythwyck, frozen solid.

'So cold,' said Colette.

'I know,' said Silver Nightly, leaning against the long table beside Colette. 'I've been thinking of warming it up a little. Just a degree or two. But it's one of those things that Madame Librarian is likely to scold me for. It's been worsening, that winter, for quite a while. But even more curious is something you'll see if you look away south. It has me a little concerned.'

Colette's eyes tracked across the Restless Sea towards the Islands of Xunchilla and beyond. She gasped. 'That doesn't look good.'

'As you can see, it runs from the heart of the desert right out to the ocean,' said Silver Nightly.

'Is that normal?' she asked. 'That worlds suddenly get great huge cracks in them?'

'I've not seen it, but then I'm still fairly new on the job. That rupture happened some time ago. The world was quite close at the time and I actually heard it,' he said. 'Made a fearful noise. It's not my place, as such, to intervene in the storytelling. Perhaps there was meant to be an earthquake. But then, when it came in for routine maintenance, I saw that winter had settled. A deep bitter winter. Now, as you can see, it's still winter and I would darn near swear it's been a year or more. And that fracture in the world, that's exactly the same as it was after it happened.'

He paused and then continued, 'It's a nasty thing, that split. It goes way down. But the strangest thing, and maybe the reason I've been keeping a close eye on it, is that the whole place has a lonesome, deserted feel. It's not right.'

'Like Brown Street,' murmured Colette.

Silver Nightly picked up another pair of spectacles and, together with Colette, peered into the world.

'I see a ship,' said Colette, spying a mast on the fierce seas.

'Well, that's a new development,' said Silver Nightly. 'I would think that is a good thing.'

'Three masts, flying a flag with a lightning bolt on it,' said Colette.

Silver Nightly nodded. 'Maybe not as deserted as I thought.'

Colette squinted and the magnifying glasses seemed to respond, focusing tightly on the deck of the ship. There was a tall green creature with bright green hair, his arms outstretched as if he'd just thrown something. And there, peering over the side of the ship, Colette was amazed to see Tuesday, in Colette's rainbow poncho. Colette was glad to see Tuesday was dressed for the weather at least. That particular poncho had accompanied Colette on many treks.

'Ah, there, in the water,' Colette said, glimpsing a flash of blue.

It had to be Vivienne Small! That was the colour of her wings! Which meant the rest of Vivienne Small was also in the sea. And putting two and two together, Colette surmised that the green creature had thrown her in.

'Oh, my,' said Silver Nightly after observing the scene for a few moments. 'Tuesday sure does know how to get herself into an adventure. But she also knows how to get herself out of one. I know it seems dangerous, but that young lady has more mettle than a cross-continent railway track.'

'I need to reach her,' said Colette, taking off the spectacles and fixing Silver Nightly with a stare. 'Can you put me in there somehow?'

Silver Nightly removed his spectacles, drawing himself up and noticing again that while he was tall, Colette was at least as tall, if not slightly taller. He shook his head. 'It's forbidden. I'm sorry to say it, but it's absolutely not allowed. This world will be going out again soon enough, and after that ... well, as you are aware there are very strict rules about entering worlds.'

'This Librarian, can she get me in?'

'She could ... but she won't.'

'I have a duty of care,' said Colette Baden-Baden. 'I gave my word that I would look after Tuesday. And I fear she may be in danger from that strange green creature.'

'Ruff, ruff,' said Baxterr.

'Yes, you could go, doggo. In fact I think you ought to go,' said Colette. 'But first, take me to this Librarian. When will this world be out there again?' she asked Silver Nightly, waving her hand at the worlds floating above the Conservatory.

'Oh, no time at all,' said Silver Nightly.

'Ruff,' said Baxterr.

Silver Nightly raised an eyebrow, but Colette did not explain.

'I would like to have been more help,' said Silver Nightly.

'I would have liked that too, Mr Gardener,' said Colette.

After only the briefest of goodbyes, Silver Nightly watched Colette and Baxterr take off into the darkness. Baxterr gave a few dips of his wings and then they were lost between worlds.

Apache gave a whine. The Gardener patted her head.

'Quite a dog. Quite a woman,' he said, and he stood there a while longer.

Chapter Twelve

Baxterr flew up and up, threading a path through the swirling worlds. He and Colette flew until only one thing remained in the sky above them: a sphere of palest mist. To Colette's intense relief, this time she and Baxterr flew easily into the mist, which seemed to her to give off a pleasant, cinnamon smell. For a moment they were enclosed in whiteness. Then they emerged on the other side of it, and Colette had a stunning aerial view of a large, white building and its beautiful formal gardens, pathways and fountains. It was early evening and the building was bathed in a large circle of light emanating from its many French windows. It had a wide stone balcony, and binoculars were mounted at intervals on the railings.

For Colette's benefit, Baxterr flew a slow lap all around the perimeter of the building, his furred wings beating the air as softly and silently as an owl's.

'*Imagine*,' she read aloud as they passed by the main entrance, for the word, as you know, was carved above the door as a direction, an invitation and a reminder.

Baxterr came in to land beyond the lit balcony and lawns where the shadows had grown long. Almost instantly he assumed his regular size. Colette smelled roses and lilac.

'Now, where do we find this Librarian?' asked Colette.

'Ruff,' said Baxterr.

'All right, we will be very quiet if you think it is necessary,' said Colette more quietly. 'But which way to do we go?'

'Doggo?' came a voice.

A tall boy was approaching them from deeper in the garden, crouching low as he made his way across the lawn. Colette observed that he was wearing filthy clothes, combat boots that were mostly unlaced, and a torn deerstalker hat. His arms and face were scratched and bruised and he was powdered with what appeared to be a fine ash, almost as if he had recently been standing close to an exploding building.

Colette watched with interest as Baxterr rushed at the boy, leapt into his arms and licked his face.

'Hush now. He is not a roast of lamb,' she said.

The boy looked at her with a slightly stern expression and Colette was reminded of one of her literary action heroes, Jack Bonner.

'So would you like to tell me where Tuesday is?' he asked curtly.

'Who's asking?' Colette replied, bristling slightly.

'Blake,' said the boy, lowering Baxterr to the ground and standing firm. 'Blake Luckhurst.'

Colette Baden-Baden stared at Blake. Her mouth fell open and no matter how hard she tried to form words in her mouth, all she could manage was a strangled sound.

'You, you ...' she managed at last. 'You are Blake Luckhurst, the author, yes?'

Blake grinned, and his persona of world-weary modern-day hero dropped from him. 'That's me.'

'I am a great fan of your books,' said Colette with intensity. 'Jack Bonner is ...'

A red flush rushed up Colette's face and she took off her hat and stared at her feet. Then she continued in her gravelly voice, her words coming fast.

'What I like is that you know the sound a bomb makes. And what people do when they are crazy with fear. You know how to get people in a big fix, and then get them out of it. You have a knack for making the heart race. You never say too much, but you do not say too little. I, well, I ...' Here Colette hesitated seemingly for once lost for words. 'I thank you for many wonderful evenings with just a lamp and a sleeping bag and a book. So young to be so talented. Ha. I am honoured to meet you.'

She held out her huge hand and Blake took it.

'Thank you, so much, Miss ...?' he said, smiling magnanimously, as if he were accustomed to this response from fans.

'I am Colette Baden-Baden,' Colette said, and Baxterr ruffed as if to confirm this with Blake. 'I am godmother to Tuesday, and a long-time friend to her mother and father.'

'Mr McGillycuddy,' said Blake, and an edge of pain came into his voice. 'He was one of a rare kind. Tragic.'

'Indeed,' said Colette. 'He was my oldest friend.'

Baxterr gave a small ruff. Blake grimaced and shook his head. 'I'm so sorry. It's been hard to know what to do. Tuesday's hardly returned my calls.'

'We are all bereft,' said Colette with a sigh. 'But there is urgent business to attend to.'

'So Tuesday ... is she here with you?' Blake asked. 'Somewhere?'

'That is why I have come to the Librarian for help,' said Colette.

'Help?' Blake said, swallowing.

'Ruff,' said Baxterr softly. 'Ruff, ruff.'

'Yes, yes, doggo,' said Colette. 'Of course you must go. You have been exceedingly patient. I will be fine from here. You go on, hmm? Go find

Tuesday and ensure she is safe. Hurry! Come back the minute you know something. Meanwhile I will find this Librarian. *Vite! Schnell!*'

Baxterr, needing no further encouragement, returned to his magnificent Winged Dog size. In one powerful, graceful movement, he sprang into the air.

Chapter Thirteen

You may think it sounds like fun to be to be whisked away from your home into another world altogether. And perhaps you understand how exciting it could be to find yourself aboard a great sailing ship speeding across a wild green sea, a strong breeze bearing you into the unknown. But I'm sure you also realise how frightening it would be to find yourself unable to get off that ship, to know that you are in fact captive to someone who seems, if not entirely mad, then certainly unpredictable and cruel.

Tuesday had just seen her dear friend – someone whose heroism she had admired for all of her reading life – trussed up, tossed overboard and possibly drowned. And for Tuesday the fact that Baxterr was not at her side was deeply unsettling. Tuesday's heart fluttered like a moth too close to a light. What was she to do? She knew – as you all know – that she was in a story. But whose story? Was she somehow creating this story? Or was it a story made by this very odd grassboy? Tuesday hunkered down against the wheelhouse, bracing herself against the motion of the rolling sea, and tried to make sense of everything.

On Tuesday's previous visits to the world of Vivienne Small, she had found the place to be just as she and her mother had imagined it. Over many years Tuesday and Serendipity had sat together in City Park, or at the kitchen table, or in Serendipity's writing room, considering the features of Vivienne Small's world. What did the Peppermint Forest look like? What did it smell like? What did it sound like? Tuesday and Serendipity had taken many walks together over the years, sometimes in far-flung places. They would climb a path through a steep pine forest, or wander through a sunlit beech forest, or stroll through a pungent rainforest, and discuss how this world and the world of Vivienne Small might be the same. They had discussed the homes and boats of Vivienne Small, and the people and animals of her world. They had discussed cities and seasons, moons and tides, time and weather.

When Tuesday was younger, Serendipity read the Vivienne Small books aloud to her, and Tuesday had always found the story world entirely familiar. Once she could read the stories herself, the world was always there waiting for her, as well known and reliable as ever, and that was part of what made the adventures so wonderful. But Loddon, here in the world of Vivienne Small, and this winter that felt far too cold: these things were entirely new.

Tuesday knew that somehow it had to make sense, but the ship was riding up over increasingly tall and steep waves, the wind was howling, and it was all making it hard to concentrate on anything except holding on. The rigging shuddered and groaned every time the boat descended the far side of a wave. Tuesday felt as if she were going to slide down the deck and slam into the railings. Or she might even be tossed overboard. It was like being on a terrifying water slide.

Loddon, however, seemed unworried. He held his arms aloft as if he were conducting the sea and the wind, which perhaps he was. His face was a mask of delighted concentration, his hair a quiff of luminous green. As Tuesday watched the ship forge through the waves, another fragment of verse came back to her.

The boy called Loddon has bright green hair,
  But if you meet him, best beware.

Was that right? she wondered. She tried to remember Serendipity reciting the poem.

Down in the garden underneath the tree,
the boy called Loddon calls to me,
The boy called Loddon has bright green hair,
best not to answer, best to leave him there …

Loddon? Who had Loddon been? And if he was Loddon, then how had he come to the world of Vivienne Small? Tuesday knew it had to make sense. Somehow it had to make sense. But no matter which way she turned it over in her mind, it didn't. Why had he called her? Why had he sent the thread to find her? What did he want with her?

And then she had a terrible realisation. Maybe he hadn't sent the thread to find *her*. After all, the thread had come to the window of her mother's writing room. Maybe he had not been looking for Tuesday at all. Maybe he'd come looking for *Serendipity*. Was that why he called Tuesday 'Writer'? Was that why he seemed so pleased to see her? Did Loddon actually think Tuesday was Serendipity? A much younger Serendipity? Did she really look so similar to her mother as a girl? She had never seen a photo of her mother as a child, so it was impossible for Tuesday to know.

'We didn't have a camera,' Serendipity had said. 'We didn't have anything.'

'You had your mum and dad,' Tuesday had said.

'Oh, yes,' her mother had sighed. 'But let's not talk about them.'

Still, Loddon had recognised Tuesday and was convinced he knew her.

The sea heaved and the ship plummeted down the next wave, then began to climb. The wind screeched about Tuesday's face and flung back the hood of her poncho at every opportunity. In each wall of water that the ship climbed, Tuesday could see seaweed and fish and strange black shapes that might have been enormous stingrays. She wondered how Vivienne was faring. She knew Vivienne Small had gotten herself out of far greater fixes than being thrown overboard, but she hadn't had such big wings back then. And those wings hadn't been sewn together. How would she swim? Tuesday felt sick again. Maybe it was the motion of the ship, or maybe it was the knowledge that it was she who had wanted Vivienne to have bigger wings. If Vivienne's new wings were the death of her, Tuesday would never forgive herself.

Tuesday wanted to lie down in her own bed, put her head on her pillow and cry. But she was here, on this ship, with this awful creature. She had to keep her wits about her, and keep scanning the sky for Baxterr. Surely he would come soon. The icy wind was vicious on her skin, burning her eyes and freezing her nose. Tuesday pulled Colette's poncho tighter around her. Surely Baxterr would find her?

Though there was no sun to guide her, Tuesday sensed the day growing old. She didn't want to be out on this turbulent sea in the dark. She stared up at the marauding grey clouds, willing Baxterr's shape to wing its way down to the ship and whisk her to safety. And then she remembered the way Vivienne had stared so deliberately up into the rigging before Loddon threw her overboard. What had she been trying to say?

Tuesday stood up and, holding on to the railing, made her way along the ship.

'Thinking of a swim, Writer?' Loddon called.

She turned and stared at him, then nonchalantly observed the rigging.

'Are you having fun, Writer? Are you ready to tell me a story?' Loddon called.

Spotting a tiny movement above, Tuesday quickly looked back into Loddon's eyes and held his gaze, all the while aware of the tiny pointed face and dark eyes she had glimpsed. *Ermengarde*, Tuesday thought, her spirits lifting to see Vivienne's rodent companion. She felt sure Loddon would not like Ermengarde, and she didn't want to take any chances. If she ever saw Vivienne Small again, she wanted to deliver Ermengarde safely back to her care.

Tuesday leaned against the mast.

'No, I'm not ready to tell you a story,' she called, and was slightly amazed that her words came out sounding as confident as they did.

After a moment, Tuesday felt Ermengarde's tiny front paws on the nape of her neck. Then her back paws before Ermengarde disappeared inside the hood of Tuesday's poncho. She was relieved that Loddon was too busy negotiating the ship over a wave to have seen a thing.

'But why won't you tell me a story?' he called.

'Well, I'm cold for one thing, and I'm hungry,' Tuesday replied, feeling Ermengarde settle on her shoulder. She raised her hand as if to rub her neck, gave Ermengarde's warm body a brief pat, then arranged the hood more closely about her neck as if to protect herself from the sea spray. 'And you just threw my friend into the sea. Why should I tell you a story at all?'

'Oh, but stories stop the hunger. They make everything better. You know that. On rainy days. Sunny days. On days when there was only shouting in the house. You didn't want to be inside. So you'd run away and stay under the tree with me and tell me stories. Stories, you said then, were even better than food because they never ran out. You promised they'd never run out.'

Tuesday frowned. She remembered her father making toasted ham-on-cheese-on-more-cheese sandwiches and her mother saying, 'Until I met your father, I actually cared nothing for food. I would have been happy to eat once a week. I much preferred writing to eating. But, eventually, his grilled cheese sandwiches won me over.'

'And my macaroni cheese,' her father had added.

'And your cheese soufflé.'

'And my cheese and chive omelette.'

Tuesday and her parents would go on, thinking of every dish Denis had ever put cheese in.

'Bolognaise with cheese. Cheese pretzels. Cheesy pizza. Cheese on bacon on ...'

'Loddon?' Tuesday asked.

'Yes?' said Loddon, and his smile was like a rainbow appearing. 'Yes, Writer?'

'Loddon, how long have I been gone?'

'Such a long time. Such a long, long, long, long time. I was down there, in my box, underneath the tree. And then the stories stopped. They just stopped. And it was lonely. I waited. I waited so long, but you forgot me, didn't you? I got hungry. I got so hungry, Writer. And then the breaking day happened.'

'The breaking day? What is the breaking day?'

'We're nearly there,' said Loddon.

'I don't understand.'

'You will,' he said.

He pointed. Ahead, Tuesday saw a shadow of steep coastline. But there was something wrong with it. It didn't resemble any coastline she had seen before. She squinted, trying to make sense of the irregular shapes and dark patches. And as the ship sailed closer, making its way right up to what had once been cliffs, Tuesday realised that the cliffs had been split open. *What kind of force could do this*? she wondered. She stared in awe at the giant rocks that lay, shattered and sheared, along the edge of the land. There were others that had tumbled into the sea, and now stood like dark icebergs among the waves. Loddon guided *Storm Rider* in between the broken cliffs

'What happened here?' Tuesday asked.

'I dug my way out. And I brought *Storm Rider* with me,' he said. 'All on my own. No one to help. No one to hear.'

In the lee of the rocks and broken cliffs, the sea was calm at last. The ship's rigging ceased its creaking and the wind subsided. The deck stopped heaving and Tuesday took a deep breath of relief.

'But what caused this?' she asked. 'Was there an earthquake?'

Loddon said nothing. His gaze was fixed ahead, navigating between the chunks of rock and rubble until Tuesday heard the ship grind against rock. *Storm Rider* had come to rest, leaning slightly to one side

'We have to go on foot from here,' he said.

'Where are we going, Loddon?' Tuesday asked.

'You know where we're going.' He smiled. His hair was brighter than ever now it wasn't being blown about by the wind. 'We're going home.'

'But, maybe I don't want to go to this … home,' said Tuesday, willing her voice to still sound strong. How would anyone find her if she went wherever Loddon was taking her? How would Baxterr find her? How would she ever find her way out?

'Ridiculous!' said Loddon. 'Home is the best place in the world. You know that. You've just forgotten. I'll lead the way.'

'Loddon, I don't want to go,' said Tuesday. She forced a smile. 'I'm happy to stay here.'

Loddon picked up a rope and wound it about his arm. He walked towards her as Tuesday took a step backwards. 'If you don't come now, I will tie you up and carry you.'

'I'll walk,' said Tuesday, raising her hands as if she gave up. 'You don't need to tie me up.'

'Down you go, then,' he said with a laugh, indicating the ladder at the side of the ship.

Tuesday reached up and rubbed her neck again, reassuring the hidden Ermengarde that everything was all right, then climbed down the ladder ahead of Loddon. The shore was dark and lustrous and as soon as Tuesday's feet touched the ground, she heard a ferocious cracking sound. A great splinter appeared at her feet and zigzagged away. The land was frozen!

'Chilly, isn't it?' said Loddon. 'But not at home. No, no, no.'

Seemingly unperturbed by the ice on his bare green feet, he scrambled ahead and tied the ship's bow rope around a large boulder that was high up on the shore.

'I will lead the way, Writer. What was that story you told me? *First star to the right then straight on 'til morning!*'

Tuesday was pretty certain it was 'second star to the right' but she did not correct Loddon as she observed that the first star had indeed appeared in the sky. Night had come. She searched keenly for a winged shadow, but all she could see was that one star amid a mass of murky clouds. It was bitterly cold and Tuesday's breath fogged ahead of her. Then she felt something gently, coldly, touch her cheek. It was a snowflake. She put out her hands and soon her palms were dotted with the tiny white slivers of snow.

'Come along, Writer,' said Loddon. 'Winter isn't leaving anytime soon.'

Tuesday stroked Ermengarde again as she pulled the hood over her head, glad for at least one small friend to be accompanying her on this strange journey.

They began to walk, Loddon leading the way. The snow was falling in earnest and the world was muffled. The only noise was that of Loddon's feet crunching against ice and fallen rock, and her own footsteps following behind. Glancing back, Tuesday saw the ship silhouetted against the dark horizon, its white sails turning grey and ghostly in the deepening snowfall.

Their path was little more than a split between two walls that got higher and higher as they went. It seemed to Tuesday that their thoroughfare had been made by something big and heavy that had passed through with enough force to push aside rocks and boulders. Tuesday wondered what this thing had been, and she was sure Loddon had something to do with it.

'C'mon, Writer,' he called again, loping ahead of her.

In that moment, Tuesday knew what every writer knows. That even though you have no idea what is going to happen next, you have to go on. And so she went on, with Ermengarde hidden on her shoulder. After a moment, another little fragment of the verse popped into her head.

The boy called Loddon underneath the tree.
I wonder if he calls to me?
I put him in a box far down below,
Down where all the stories go.

'I'm okay,' she whispered. 'You're okay,' she said to Ermengarde. 'We're both okay.'

Chapter Fourteen

Tuesday followed Loddon along the crevasse away from the sea. As they walked, the night darkened and the snow thickened until they had to wade through it. After a long time, the deep crevasse ended in the black mouth of a tunnel.

'Here we are,' said Loddon. He flourished a hand at the tunnel entrance.

'In there?' Tuesday asked.

'Down, down below,' said Loddon.

Tuesday peered around, searching for some-where else, anywhere else, to go. But there was nowhere else. So she stepped into the tunnel.

Inside, it was eerily quiet. Tuesday could hear her heartbeat echoing in her ears.

'Down below. You know. Just the way you imagined it,' Loddon said, taking the lead again.

The tunnel had score marks in the ceiling and a single deep rut in the floor. The walls were smooth as if a giant earthmover had scoured them away. Loddon, Tuesday discovered, gave off a faint glow in the gloom, and his smell – a rich, fetid smell – became apparent. Still, the glow was welcome. It was like having a giant glow-worm walking ahead of her.

When they came to a sheer and icy wall, Tuesday at last understood what had produced this tunnel. The enormous outline of *Storm Rider* was imprinted in the fractured remains of the wall. Tuesday realised that Loddon must have dragged the huge sailing ship up out of the earth, towing it behind him as he walked. Tuesday felt a chill climb her spine. Just how strong *was* this grassboy?

Then something else in the ice wall caught Tuesday's eye. She stared, then wiped her hand across the freezing, glassy surface. Buried deep inside she glimpsed a large, pale page printed with a few enormous blurry words. It was as if someone had magnified a page from a menu. She made out the beautiful script: *Crème Brûlée*. Below that *Mousse au Chocol* ... but the rest of the word must have broken away when Loddon hacked his way through. Eyes wide, Tuesday continued on through the ship-shaped tunnel, a few steps behind Loddon. A little further on, poking out of another ice wall, were the remains of a flickering pink neon sign. It read: *Sweet Cactus*. After that, Tuesday came across an enormous record player. The needle was still on a record, as if the music were still playing.

On the far side of an ice fissure that seemed to reach down into an infinite darkness, Tuesday discovered a giant pink suit jacket frozen into a puddle. Something about the jacket made Tuesday feel terribly sad. It reminded her of her father, and she realised that with everything that had happened since leaving Brown Street, she had hardly thought about Denis at all. At times over the past year, Tuesday had tried to teach herself not to think about her father. But she had discovered that not thinking about someone was sometimes more painful than thinking about them. So, she gave herself over to thinking what Denis would make of all this.

'It's a magical mystery, Tuesday. It's a chilling thriller. Ice is not always nice. It's winter and the walls of the world are all awry. Keep your wits about you. It's a puzzle, but possibly not an impossible one.'

Instinctively Tuesday reached up and stroked the warm bundle of Ermengarde at the nape of her neck. The little rat sniffed at her hand and Tuesday felt her teeth gently nibbling her fingers.

'I'm hungry too,' she murmured.

Tuesday found, wedged in a ruptured wall of ice, a bright orange dancing shoe that was several times larger than it ought to be. Then a huge cup with a broken handle and a picture of a camel on its side. Not far after the cup there appeared an enormous set of skis, and much further on – after she had followed Loddon across fissures and skirted crevices and clambered over rocks where the tunnel had subsided – there was an over-sized daisy chain hanging from a curve of wall. When Tuesday reached out to touch it, she realised the flower was made of paper.

Countless times, Tuesday had asked how much further would it be, and when they would get there, and where were they going, but all she had received from Loddon was the same infuriating answer.

'I had to come such a long way to find you, Writer.'

Tuesday couldn't decide whether this was more or less irritating than his constant humming. 'Hm hm hm, nee nee nee, ni ni ni neee, hmmmm, wa wa waaa ...'

After a while, he broke into a fragment of verse, struggling to find the words.

I am Loddon, underneath the tree,
I can't see you, if you can't see me.
I am hidden underneath the tree,
Have you come to visit me?
I can see me, I can ...
See see see, me, me, me,
Down in the garden, underneath the tree ...

He turned back to Tuesday. 'What comes next, Writer?'

'I don't know and I won't know until we get there.'

He shrugged, and then resumed his tuneless humming. In order to drown it out, Tuesday began whistling, which made her feel strangely happy.

The tunnel was narrowing, the walls and ceiling gradually closing in. Tuesday could still see the deep groove the keel had made in the path, and the marks the rigging had left in the ceiling above, but it was as if *Storm Rider* had been smaller down here. The ice was melting and leaking, creating puddles in the path and small rivers in the walls. Tuesday poked her tongue out and tasted a little waterfall. It was slightly salty, but not bitter. She slurped at it, grateful for the moisture in her mouth. Allowing Loddon to go on ahead of her, she lifted Ermengarde out from under her poncho and offered her the water. The little black rat drank some, then looked about, her whiskers quivering. Tuesday tucked her back inside her poncho and they went on, ever downwards, and deeper into the earth.

Strangely, though, Tuesday had a sense that instead of it becoming darker as they went on, there was actually more light to see by. A pale gleam was seeping towards them from further down the tunnel and the green glow about Loddon was dimming. And Tuesday felt warmer. Soon, she slipped back her hood, and then took off the poncho altogether, draping it around her neck like a beach towel, arranging Ermengarde safely within it.

The pathway was narrowing further. Soon the tunnel was hardly taller than Loddon. The remnant items that emerged from the walls, or poked out of the ceiling and floor were more life-size. Here was a blue wooden truck, and here a party hat with one or two sparkles still clinging to its blue surface. Tuesday stopped and gently peeled away part of the wall. What she held in her hand was a page from a book. Whatever had been written on it had blurred beyond recognition. Only the faint remnant of an illustration remained: a tree house in a forest.

The ice-melt and dampness were gone. Now the tunnel was dry and Tuesday could no longer see evidence of the ship at all. Instead, the tunnel looked as if it had been bored out by a large digging animal. Tuesday stared at Loddon's back. Had he really dug all this way?

The further they went, the more paper Tuesday found. The wall she was passing was made of an arc of brittle, yellowed notebooks. Soon the walls were made entirely of layer after layer of paper.

What is this place? she wondered.

'It's a positively perplexing problem to ponder,' she heard Denis say in her head.

'What am I going to do, Dad?' she asked. 'How am I ever going to get back to the surface again?'

'A question comes before an answer,' said Denis. 'All pathways lead somewhere.'

Loddon dropped to his hands and knees ahead of her, and Tuesday hoped the tunnel didn't get any smaller. It was clear, though, that they were moving towards a bright circle of light. Tuesday took a deep breath and crawled after Loddon through a narrow opening to emerge in a vast, bright cavern.

'Welcome back, Writer,' Loddon said with a deep bow.

The space he gestured to was enormous, easily big enough to hold three or four houses. But instead it held staircases: narrow white staircases, without bannisters or railings. They wound up and up, spiralling, intersecting and then separating. Some of the staircases spanned the arc of the cavern's high ceiling, crossing and recrossing each other in alarmingly precarious ways. Some of the staircases led to dark openings in the walls. Caves, Tuesday surmised. Others stopped abruptly, or a frightening distance short of the cave entrances, as if you were simply meant to jump.

Growing in the floor of the cavern, beneath all these paper staircases, was a spectacular tree with pale bark and deep green foliage. Hanging from one of its outstretched limbs was a rubber tyre swing. The grass that grew in the cavern was tall and exactly the green of Loddon's hair. Sunflowers burst upwards, and other flowers dotted the grass with reds, purples, yellows and blues. Above the tree, in the midst of the highest staircases, hung a great orange and yellow sun with pointed tips, glowing and spinning slowly in a faint breeze. There were also clouds and several birds in flight. But all of it, everything, the staircases, the tree, the flowers, the sun, the clouds and grass, it was all, Tuesday realised, made of ... paper.

Chapter Fifteen

After the Librarian left her at the boatshed, Serendipity kicked off her boots, curled up on the bed, pulled the counterpane over herself and slept. She slept and slept, and her sleep went on, deep and dreamless, for a very long time.

When she awoke, the sun was creeping in over the lake, streaking the sky with persimmon red and tangerine orange. She gazed at the sunrise, watching the sky change. It softened into the palest of pinks, and finally became the sort of blue it would be wonderful to paint a room. Serendipity sighed and stretched and thought about a morning walk. On the kitchen table she observed a green pear that she was sure had not been there the day before. She listened and could hear only the songs of birds and the quietest lap of water on the pebbled shore. She picked up the pear and opened the glass door onto the balcony. There were steps leading down to the lake on either side and Serendipity considered if she should go right, or left. Her feet seemed to decide for her, and she went left.

She ambled along the shore, noting reeds and rocks, reflections in the water and birds in the sky. She breathed deeply several times, as if she had almost forgotten how to breathe, and there was something about the simplicity of a walk by a lake, after a night spent far from home, that seemed to awaken in her a sense of something new. She couldn't quite place the feeling. It was a little bit heavy and a little bit fizzy all at once.

She was unable to tell if minutes or hours had passed, but at some point Serendipity found herself back at the boatshed. She ate, although she couldn't have said what she ate, and she slept. The next time she awoke it was sunrise again and again there was a green pear on the table. She went for a walk and listened to birds and watched tiny flies skim the lake surface and every now and then a fish would rise and snap a fly.

I should be home, she thought. *Or, Tuesday should be here.*

But almost immediately she heard the Librarian's voice saying, '*Perhaps your daughter is beginning something. Best not get in the way.*' And Colette saying, '*Everyone here will be safe. You have my word.*'

And so Serendipity walked and slept, and time went by. It might have been days, or it might have been weeks, and how much time that might be back at Brown Street, Serendipity had no way of knowing. Perhaps only a single night. Tuesday was with Colette and Colette would take care of her. Of that, she was certain.

One morning Serendipity found herself taking a notebook with her as she went for her walk on the shore. Along the lakeside, where up until now there had been only forest, she found a white gate, the paint flaking and the hinges rusted. She pushed it open. There was a path leading to a garden where the grass was long and several pear trees were heavy with fruit.

She blinked and breathed deeply. She knew this place. Far back down the garden she saw the house with its peeling blue paint and sagging porch. The porch was strung with macramé plant holders, and the plants they held were wilting. The back door was open and a radio was playing inside the house. Serendipity made her way across the garden and climbed the creaking back stairs. One cat was sitting on the windowsill while another reclined on a torn sofa.

Inside the house a woman was sitting at the kitchen table, her head bowed, her fingers working a length of string for another plant holder.

'Hello, Mum,' said Serendipity.

Serendipity had not seen her mother for many years. Her mother had died just after Serendipity had met Denis. But here she was, and everything was just the same. The bare floor and faded green bench tops. The stale smell of cobwebs and mouse poo. There was the table littered with lengths of string. The brown radio on the ledge above the sink. The sound of her father's snoring coming from down the hall, though it was daytime.

Serendipity opened the fridge and saw that it was empty except for a wedge of old cabbage.

'There's nothing to eat, so don't ask,' said her mother sharply, not looking up from her work. 'And if you wake your father, you know what will happen.'

Serendipity went outside, closing the screen door very quietly behind her. She walked through the long green grass to the rear of the garden and lay under the pear tree. She felt terribly hungry suddenly, as if she hadn't eaten for days. She remembered how she had made a boy out of grass. She hadn't thought of him in years, but suddenly she shivered and sat up. Clouds raced across the sun.

'Loddon,' she whispered.

He was silhouetted against the light.

'Hello, Writer,' he said.

She realised she had grown small. She was a child again, wearing a thin nightdress. Her feet were bare and smudged with dirt. Her stomach rumbled with emptiness. She opened the notebook and began to write a story, adding drawings from time to time. Loddon slumped down beside her.

'I'm hungry,' he said. 'Tell me a story.'

'When I'm finished,' she said.

At last, she read the story aloud to the grassboy she had made.

'But that's not about me!'

'Of course it's not. It's about Captain Mothwood and I'm going to write lots of stories about him.'

'But you have to write about me!'

'I've written heaps of stories about you.'

'I don't like Mothwood,' said Loddon, snatching away the notebook and tearing out the pages, then he stuffed them into his pockets.

'Ha ha,' he said, laughing. 'Now you have to write another one.'

'Why do you always want more?'

'Because I'm hungry,' he said. 'Tell me a story. Tell me another story.'

'I will,' she said, sighing. Her own hunger had vanished. It felt as if she had eaten a good meal. 'Just give me back my notebook.'

She grabbed at the notebook, but Loddon grew taller and taller, a silhouette against the afternoon sky, and she could hear her own voice from far away calling, 'Loddon, Loddon, don't be mean. Why do you have to be mean?'

When Serendipity woke up, she was back in the boatshed under the white counterpane, and the sun was rising again.

Chapter Sixteen

The sun also rose, weak and pale, in the world of Vivienne Small. And there, on the sand of an islet in the deepest reaches of the Restless Sea, lay something that could easily have been mistaken for a large, blue and storm-battered butterfly. It had been washed up on the tide line where the sand was gritty and damp, its ragged and waterlogged wings pressed together, and its body curled against the cold. Night came. A day passed, and then another night. And still this creature remained absolutely still, except for when a gust of icy wind caused a tiny flutter at the very edges of its wings.

Vivienne Small's lips and cheeks were almost the same shade of blue as her painfully stitched-up wings. Most of Loddon's stitches had held, but here and there the leathery skin of Vivienne's wings had torn through the thread.

But Vivienne did not move. Was she alive, or dead? She hardly knew herself. When at long last her eyes fluttered open and took in glimpses of a tilting landscape of sea and sand, she could not feel her frozen arms or legs, and the weight of her waterlogged wings pinned her upper body to the ground. And then came flashes of memory. Or a dream? Of being hurled through the air under a sky full of scudding cloud. Mountains of white-veined water. Bitter cold. The silence. Then falling down, down, through layers of deepening darkness. She had not panicked. Vivienne Small did not, as a rule, panic. Had her wings been able to move freely, they would have helped her in the manner of a manta ray's fins, but stitched together as they were, they dragged uselessly, an impediment as she kicked towards the distant sheen of light. But kick she did. At last, through

sheer determination and ferocity, she surfaced
and gasped for life.

Treading water, she had turned slow circles,
searching for any sign of solid ground or hope.
There was nothing to see but water: a cold,
mountainous swell of water that slowly carried
away from her the last of her body's warmth
and strength and plunged her into strange and
dangerous moments of sleep. She floated then,
staring at the grey sky, knowing the sea had a way
of returning things to shore.

A little more awake now, on the sand, Vivienne
shuddered. Somehow she had made it to land.
Pins and needles started up violently in her arms
and hands, legs and feet. Her head throbbed.
She succeeded in moving her uppermost wing
and felt a spear of pain travel through her. She
breathed the pain in and, with a little growl of
determination, defied it. Then she slumped back
to the sand and thought of Ermengarde.

'I could seriously use your help,' Vivienne
whispered, thinking of how swiftly her rat's

sharp teeth could have undone Loddon's horrible handiwork.

'Stop complaining, Vivienne,' she told herself. 'Get up and get moving.'

And so, more with strength of mind than strength of body, she forced herself to sit up. The pain and effort made her dizzy, so she sat for a moment with her head upon her leather-clad knees, until everything stopped spinning. Then she took off her boots, emptied them of water, peeled off her socks and wrung them out. Reluctantly she put them all back on. She got unsteadily to her feet, and stumbled up the beach to higher ground.

The islet was very small. It was rimmed with stretches of sand and rocky outcrops. In the centre of the islet rose a huddle of trees almost entirely stripped of their wide, fronded leaves, indicating to Vivienne the terrible gales that must have lashed through here during this long and bitter winter. At the base of the trees were smaller, more delicate plants. Or, at least, the remnants of them. Vivienne could see that their soft, lettuce-like leaves had been frozen, and then partly thawed, reducing them to clumps of withered slime.

Entering the shelter of the trees, Vivienne felt relief to be out of the chilling wind. She stepped groggily, trying to put her senses on high alert. Who lived here? What creatures made this remote islet their dwelling place? Might the trees be home to a bird that could carry a message? But though she listened, and sniffed, and had to lie down when dizziness passed through her, she could not feel the presence of another living animal or bird. But she did find something. Concealed within the ring of trees was a small, freshwater pool, its surface frosted over with ice. Vivienne used a rock to crack a small hole and, with cupped hands, slurped the cold, sweet water. She could feel it coursing down her salted throat, and running into her stomach. She could also feel the way it cleared her mind and her thoughts.

Now that she was seeing and thinking a little more clearly, she noticed a pikwan vine creeping around the trunk of one of the far trees. Her stomach rumbled even as her heart leapt. Using the same rock, she tapped open the prickly case of a pikwan. The fruit inside was shrivelled, but she put it into her mouth regardless. She had to chew hard, and the flesh tasted sour. But it was food, and that, Vivienne reasoned, was better than nothing.

Several bitter pikwans later, Vivienne Small stepped out from under the cover of the trees, onto the deserted beach where she had washed up. The light had fallen, as if the sun had edged away a little further from the world. In every direction there was nothing to see but ocean, and a low, thunderous sky. No birds, no sea animals, no hope, no nothing … except … a distant shape.

Vivienne blinked. There was something aloft, though it was barely visible against the steel-blue clouds. It was very far from her, but coming a little closer, she thought. It flew as if it were searching for something. It glided on outspread wings, and then made a few wing-beats before gliding again, its eyes scanning the water. Whatever it was, it was hunting. And it was huge.

Could it be? Vivienne wondered. *Was it possible?*

'Doggo?' she yelled. 'Doggo! Is that you? HERE! I'm here!' But surely the creature was much too far away to hear her. 'Doggo!' she called again. 'I'm here!'

It was coming her way, and fast, as if it had heard her. Vivienne watched, spellbound, as moments later Baxterr landed on the beach, dwarfing the islet with his magnificent wingspan. Vivienne felt tears of happiness and relief gathering in her eyes, but brushed them away crossly. Baxterr gave Vivienne a tremendous lick that covered her from knees to forehead. It was wet, but it was also warm, in more ways than one.

'You wonderful, wonderful dog!' Vivienne said, hugging one of his ankles.

'Ruff,' said Baxterr.

'We have to rescue Tuesday,' Vivienne said. 'And Ermengarde.'

'Ruff,' Baxterr agreed.

'They're in terrible danger. They're with that vile, green *grassboy*!' Vivienne said.

Vivienne wasted no time, taking thick handfuls of fur to pull herself up onto Baxterr's shoulders, continuing to tell Baxterr all that had happened. Settled into the plush depths of his fur, Vivienne could feel Baxterr's warmth coursing through her veins. The relief was palpable. Baxterr spread his wings and in a few powerful beats they were aloft, climbing up into the sky. Vivienne gave the islet a brief nod of thanks, for when she cast her gaze below, it was the only speck of land she could see.

Chapter Seventeen

'Story time!' said Loddon, gesturing for Tuesday to sit on the paper swing.

Tuesday found it hard to move. She was unable to stop staring at the terrifying staircases that climbed so high above her. The grass came almost up to her waist, the tall paper stalks making a crisp swishing sound as she passed, although they sprang straight back in the wake of her footsteps. Gingerly, she sat down on the swing, which felt surprisingly sturdy.

Loddon threw himself in the grass, rolled about and laughed. Tuesday frowned. Loddon had grown smaller since they had arrived in the cave. He was now about the same height as her, or possibly even shorter.

'Give me three choices,' he said.

'Choices?' Tuesday tried to swallow and realised her mouth was parched. She and Loddon had walked such a long way, and such a long time had passed. Every part of her was sure it was actually night, not this strange paper daytime. The last drink she'd had was from the little waterfall in the tunnel, and she was sure that had been hours ago. She knew Ermengarde must also need water.

'Loddon, I will have to sleep first. And I need water. And food.'

'Food?' said Loddon, frowning. 'Not food. Stories. Three choices.'

'I don't remember this game, Loddon.'

Loddon rolled onto his stomach and stared at the grass in front of him. In a peevish voice he said, 'You're just being mean. You give me three titles and I tell you which story I want. That's why you're a writer. You are meant to tell stories.'

Tuesday thought. She wanted desperately to have quiet time, thinking time, so she could begin to puzzle all this out. And she was so tired.

'Sometimes the answer is in the question,' she heard Denis say.

'The Girl Who Forgot, The Tree at the Bottom of the Garden, and, um …' Tuesday thought a little desperately. 'The Marbles and the Parsnip.'

'No, no, no, no, no,' said Loddon, pummelling the grass. 'No, no, no, no, no.'

Tuesday blinked and frowned.

'Where's my story? Where's my story?' Loddon raged.

'Loddon, I'm very tired. Can't we do this after—'

Loddon jumped to his feet. 'I have waited all this time. I had to dig my way out! You'd never have come back. You would've left me here forever!'

Tuesday glanced at the tunnel where they'd entered the cave. Somehow Loddon had dug his way up and into Vivienne Small's world, all the while growing bigger, and the ship he carried with him had grown bigger too. Perhaps, she thought, *Storm Rider* had been no bigger than a bath toy when he started out.

'Vivienne Small and the City of Clocks?' suggested Tuesday.

Loddon's green eyes flashed a more violent shade of green.

'Do you want me to be hungry, Writer?'

'No, Loddon,' said Tuesday, her voice barely a whisper.

'You will go to your house,' he said. 'And when you come out, you will tell me a story.'

'My house?' Tuesday asked.

'Up there,' said Loddon. He indicated the vaulted cavern. Then, seeing the expression on her face, he jumped up and beckoned for her to follow him. Loddon took to the stairs as a goat takes to a mountain. But Tuesday had never liked heights, especially not heights from narrow rickety staircases that are made of books and have no railings. Her heart pounded as she followed Loddon higher and higher. She didn't want to look down, but nor did she want to look up. Her palms were sweating. At one point she simply sank to her knees and clung to the sides of the steps until her vision cleared.

How Loddon knew quite which staircase to

take, she didn't know, but he flitted ahead of her, waiting with his arms folded impatiently, as she tried to keep up. In places where the staircases turned into bridges with sheer drops on either side, Tuesday found it best to walk with her arm outstretched like a tightrope walker's. And then, when the staircases became horribly thin and steep, she felt safest if she crawled. At last she heard Loddon's footsteps stop and glanced up. They had come to one of the dark openings high in the cavern wall.

'Come out when you're ready to behave,' said Loddon. Then he was past her and running down the stairs as if he had done it all his life.

Inside was a pale cave. On the far side, a small tunnel appeared to lead to more rooms. Tuesday thought about exploring, but she was too tired. So stayed where she was. The cave was about the size of her bedroom at Brown Street, although it was entirely unfurnished. But it had a single window – an opening – that offered a view of the cavern below. Tuesday could see the tree under the maze of staircases, but she couldn't see Loddon. The light in the cavern had dimmed, and she saw that the paper sun had been replaced by a curve of pale moon. There were also gold paper stars, some of them quite close to her window. She shook her head. What was this place?

The light inside the cave flickered and dimmed as if there was a lantern burning softly. Carefully, Tuesday drew Ermengarde out and stroked her. She pulled the poncho close about them both and caught its scent of wood smoke and pine needles and wondered where Colette had been for it to smell like this. She stared out at the single gold star she could glimpse from where she sat. Her eyes closed and her stomach rumbled. She imagined sitting at the kitchen table at Brown Street and eating a bowl of chicken noodle soup.

'You must be hungry too, Ermengarde,' she said. The rat nibbled gently at Tuesday's fingers as she stroked her.

Then Tuesday became aware of something sharp sticking into her leg. Her fingers searched the cave floor but it was smooth. Then she felt along the poncho. Whatever it was, it was in the fabric. Reaching inside the poncho, she discovered a tiny pocket. A small foil wrapper was partly piercing the fabric. She drew the wrapper out and observed a picture of an orange, or perhaps a mandarin, that was dancing in flaming red shoes.

Tuesday tore open the wrapper and put the contents in her mouth. A rich taste of citrus melted on her tongue. Bliss, Tuesday thought. And then she bit the sweet and a gush of liquid filled her mouth. Tuesday gasped. It was as if she'd just eaten a red hot chilli. She jumped up and fanned her tongue. The heat went on and on in waves of intensity. Tuesday flapped her hands, dancing about, moaning and groaning, her eyes streaming. She looked desperately about for something to cool her mouth, panting rapidly to quench the blaze on her tongue. Ermengarde, rather alarmed at all this, buried herself back in the poncho.

Tuesday's eyes fell upon a shadow on the wall in the far corner of the cave. She put her hand against it and discovered it was moist. She laid her tongue against it, intensely grateful for the cool damp, and made a low *aaaaah* sound. At last the heat subsided and she slid down the wall to the floor, drying her eyes. Her tongue felt like metal on a hot day, but the worst was over.

She returned Ermengarde to her shoulder and began to carefully explore the poncho, discovering that it concealed a great many little pockets. Some were empty, but some were not. Gradually Tuesday extracted a small trove of items that she laid out on the floor. There was a tiny pocket knife. Several packets of nuts. Three small pouches of dried apples. Four squares of what looked like chocolate. And a drinking straw curled up like a snail.

Tuesday took the knife to the damp section of wall and sliced a narrow channel into it. She fashioned a crude bowl at the base of the channel and waited. Soon enough, a steady drip began and after a little while she was able to use the drinking straw to slurp out the small puddle of water. It tasted a little salty but also sweet, like the water in the tunnel. She held Ermengarde while the rat poked her long nose into the bowl and sipped gratefully.

As Tuesday waited for the water bowl to refill, she shared one of the packets of nuts with

Ermengarde, who ate daintily. Next they ate a single piece of dried apple and a single square of chocolate. Every mouthful felt like a gift. Tuesday drank from the water bowl again, using her straw. She thought this was possibly one of the best meals she had ever eaten. When the bowl was empty again, she spread the poncho on the floor and wrapped herself in it, Ermengarde tucked in beside her.

'I don't know where we are, and I don't know what Loddon's plans are,' she murmured to her little companion, 'but I know Baxterr will find us somehow.'

Tuesday's eyes closed, as did Ermengarde's. Half a heartbeat later, they were asleep on the floor of the cave while outside in the cavern, the paper moon gave off a pearlescent glow, and the gold paper stars twinkled in the darkness.

Chapter Eighteen

Colette Baden-Baden stood behind a large, flowering shrub and surveyed the Library.

'So,' said Colette to Blake Luckhurst. 'Can you take me to this Librarian? If it would not be too much of an inconvenience. I can see by your appearance that you are in the midst of important business.'

Blake surveyed his dust-covered clothes and blackened hands. 'I'm not sure Madame Librarian is the person either of us wants to see,' said Blake, his voice low.

'But I was assured by the Gardener that she

was the only person who could help,' whispered Colette.

'The Gardener?' whispered Blake. 'Wow, you've been travelling about!'

'Not exactly, I fell ... well, I fell into his home.'

Blake nodded. 'You fell into ...? Interesting. And how exactly did that happen? I mean, I'm just guessing here, but you're not a writer, are you?'

'I do not write fiction,' said Colette. 'I sometimes write reports and reviews and essays ...'

'Yes, yes,' said Blake. 'But not stories.'

'I am a documentary filmmaker. I do tell stories and, until this very evening, I have always found truth to be more interesting than fiction. Other than in ...' Colette glanced sideways at Blake, '... the most engaging novels.'

'Thank you,' said Blake modestly. 'But I don't think you should be here. This is a place for writers. This is a place where writers visit their worlds and experience everything they need to write their stories. You need to leave before the Librarian catches you.'

'But that's impossible. For one thing, my trusty steed is gone, leaving me with no means of return. But even if return were possible, I made a sacred promise to Tuesday's mother that I would take care of Tuesday. And I understand the Librarian is the only person who can help me fulfil that duty right now.'

Blake shook his head slowly. 'I don't think she'll see it that way.'

'Well, I think I will go and find her and explain my circumstances. One woman to another. We will come to an understanding.'

'Why are you so sure Tuesday needs your help? I mean, Baxterr will find her. She'll be fine.'

'I have reason to believe that she is not fine. She called for help as she was pulled out the window. Baxterr is of the firm belief that she is in great danger, and I would never doubt that dog's instincts.'

'Okay, said Blake, glancing covertly once more towards the Library then sinking to sit on a stone ledge. Colette sat beside him. 'But surely Baxterr will bring her back?'

'Then I will wait. And if he does not return swiftly, then we must find this Librarian.'

'Okay,' said Blake. 'Then we'll wait together.'

And so they waited. Blake asked after the Gardener, and Colette described all that had happened during her time in the Conservatory. The night deepened and mist continued to shroud the edges of the garden and balcony. Baxterr did not reappear.

'I gather you know all about the family?' asked Colette.

Blake tilted his head. 'A bit.' He had been sworn to secrecy, and even if Colette *was* Tuesday's godmother, he was not going to reveal that he knew about the world's most famous writer and the double life she lived as the rather ordinary Sarah McGillycuddy. Not unless Colette did so first.

Colette laughed. 'I think anyone who knows Baxterr is a Winged Dog knows many other things he keeps secret. I admire that. You might be surprised to know that it was me who first suggested to Serendipity that she invent a disguise. Long ago when everybody knew her as Sarah! What do you think of that?'

Blake nodded, conceding that he was a little impressed.

'You know,' Colette continued, 'I have seen fame do terrible things to people.'

'*Really?*' said Blake.

'Oh, yeeesss. She and Denis were young. They wanted a family. I mean, how is one meant to raise a family with journalists peering through the letterbox, spying with their cameras, wanting to follow you into the supermarket? Believe me. I know. I was a journalist for many years before I became a filmmaker. It's no way for a child to be raised. And I was certain that Sarah's books would make her famous. It required planning. Well, as you know, it worked. They had a normal life when they needed it. Tuesday had a normal childhood. But now, of course, nothing is normal.'

Colette sighed grimly, struck by the truth of her statement.

'There might be another way,' Blake said. 'Into the world of Vivienne Small.'

'Yes?' Colette's eyes widened, and then narrowed.

Blake said, 'Jack Bonner always has a back-up plan.' But in truth Blake was not so certain about the one that was forming in his mind. There was only the slimmest chance of it succeeding.

'Ah! Jack Bonner,' said Colette. 'The man who says *there is no substitute for explosive force!* No, I do not think we ought to blast our way into this world. *Leave no trace* is my preferred method.'

Blake raised his binoculars and muttered, 'What's she waiting for? Surely she can't know we're here?'

In a low tone, Colette said, 'She worries you, this Librarian.'

'I've blown a deadline. I'm in a mess. She'll be furious if she catches me … but if we wait a bit longer she'll hopefully retire for the night and we can kill two birds with one stone.'

'Indeed,' said Colette. 'If reaching Tuesday's predicament is one of these birds, what is the other?'

'Food,' said Blake. 'I've been living on dehydrated potato for weeks.'

Over the course of his career, Blake had spent many a night in the great Library and not one of them had been comfortable. Sometimes he was only wounded. Other times – worse times – he was clueless and plot-less as well. He'd discovered that when you wrote action thrillers, the odds of getting injured in explosions, or crossfire, were high. And the risk of your plot going off the rails was roughly equivalent to the risk of your high-speed train doing the same thing. Being here again, he felt an old, familiar unease. Not only was the Library a vast repository for every book ever written, it was a place where books incubated, biding their time, being deliberated on by writers over months and years, waiting on shelves in strange states of transparency and translucency. And it was the Librarian's home.

She looked mild enough, as Librarians often did in his experience. She was petite and certainly not young. In fact, it was possible she was ancient. But that wasn't what bothered him. What unsettled him was her voice. It had an effect on him like no one else's, reducing him to a nervous, obedient little boy. And she had an unnerving way of discovering him whenever he had hidden himself away somewhere hoping for a brief respite. He was dreading hearing her voice at any moment, dreading her appearing in the garden in a lavender-coloured dressing-gown to berate him for sneaking about in the dark with a non-writer and an out-of-control novel.

'Do *you* think Baxterr is coming back?' asked Colette.

'He sure is taking a long time. I think we ought to figure out a way to find out what's going on. And if my plan works—' He broke off, then whispered, 'Yessss! She's switched off the main lights. Now, stay close, and *quiet*.'

Crouching low, Blake scooted out from behind the vegetation and skirted the fountain. Colette jammed her hat in her pocket, and followed. Like two shadows they tiptoed along the balcony that wrapped around the stone building. Blake slid along the wall until he reached the only pair of French windows still illuminated. Dropping to the ground, he commando-crawled along the width of the doors. He scrambled to his feet on the other side and beckoned urgently to Colette.

Colette, however, walked quietly right up to the edge of the window, and peeped inside. On the far side of the room, nestled comfortably on a mauve chaise longue that was piled with cushions, was a very small, very old woman. She was wearing a violet satin dressing-gown over matching pyjamas, and she was knitting what appeared to be a fluffy purple scarf. Her tortoiseshell needles moved fast and a skein of purple wool rolled across the mauve carpet as she tugged on it. Colette couldn't help it. She gave a little snort of laughter, then removed her hat from her pocket and pulled it down over her head and slipped – a furry shadow – past the French windows.

'You took a serious risk,' said Blake.

'That little lady is your ferocious Librarian?' she whispered to Blake, and although it was dark, she could tell he was blushing the same shade of red that his deerstalker hat might have been before it got covered in dirt and dust.

'You have no idea,' Blake said.

They continued along the balcony past the brass binoculars. Colette edged over and examined one set of these binoculars closely. She ran a finger over the coin slot on the top and automatically felt through the pockets of her coat for loose change.

'You won't have the right currency,' Blake told her. 'Trust me. Madame L dishes out the coins. But if we're lucky ...'

'What would I see, though, if I had a coin? Not this mist, eh?'

'Depends who you are,' Blake said. 'Serendipity would see the world of Vivienne Small. So would Tuesday. It's unusual – rare – but Serendipity and Tuesday share that world. Drives Madame L nuts. And me? I'd see the world of Jack Bonner.'

'Let me get this straight. You see your whole world? The whole thing? All of it? In my mind this world of Jack Bonner is very large.'

'Yeah, you see it all, to start with. But then you kind of think yourself into the exact part you need to visit. Then it appears. And see those stairs?' Blake pointed to wide, curving marble staircase that led down, apparently into the garden. 'That's the way. For a writer, that is.'

'And for those of us not so fortunate?' Colette asked.

'An abyss, I'm guessing. But follow me,' said Blake.

Chapter Nineteen

Blake, with painstaking care, twisted the handle on one of the darkened French doors and led Colette into the building. Once inside, Colette put her hands on her hips and surveyed the room. She was in a dining room with a high ceiling and a polished floor. There were a great many tables, all cloaked in white linen and softly lit by beautiful, egg-like lanterns in their centres.

Despite being on a surreptitious mission, Blake could not resist sneaking over to the buffet to see what was on offer under the silver domes that rested there.

'You can take what you like?' Colette murmured, coming up behind Blake.

'Madame L believes in writing on a full stomach,' Blake said.

IT'S A LONG NIGHT read one of the labels and under its dome was a large bowl of sugar-coated Turkish delight. Another of the labels read ENERGY REQUIRED and when Blake lifted the dome, his eyes lit up at the sight of huge, paper-wrapped souvlaki. Colette investigated the dome labelled LOSING HOPE to discover a tray of tall glasses, containing frothy ice-cream spiders. Beside each glass was a long spiral of raspberry liquorice and a red-and-white-striped drinking straw. Colette lifted a glass, sipped once, discovered it was sarsaparilla flavour, and then consumed the entire drink. She finished with a truncated slurp through her straw as Blake stuck his finger to his lips and hissed at her.

'This Madame L cannot be all bad,' Colette murmured, and began to chew on the raspberry liquorice.

Blake took an enormous mouthful of souvlaki, pocketed the rest and grabbed a handful of Turkish delight, then led the way out of the dining room and into a vast high-ceilinged entrance hall. In the low light, Colette could just make out the elegance of its paintings and side tables, but Blake was heading for a set of double doors.

'The book room,' he whispered, carefully opening one door and sliding sideways into the room beyond.

Colette followed Blake and stared. She wondered just how many times in one day she could be completely gobsmacked. Hanging from a ceiling that was almost as far away as the sky were green-shaded lights. They glowed softly, lighting the many rows of leather-topped desks. But the bookshelves! They rose, and rose, stretching away, away, away into the distance. Colette could almost hear the millions upon millions of voices all whispering their stories inside the covers of the books. The books! How many were there?

'Every story ever written,' murmured Blake. 'All eight of mine, over there in the L section. But what we've come for is *that*.'

Blake was pointing to an unprepossessing silver platform. It had railings on three sides and was resting on the floor, doing precisely nothing.

You may remember this platform. You may remember how the Librarian used it to give Tuesday her first tour of the Library, and how they dived and soared from the As to the Zs. Indeed, years before, Serendipity Smith had stood upon that platform as a young writer taking in the marvels of the great Library. As far as Blake Luckhurst knew, he and Silver Nightly – now the Gardener – were the only people who had ever accompanied the Librarian on the platform on a journey beyond the Library. On that occasion, they had dropped through the trapdoor in the Librarian's study, and into a universe of teeming worlds, a sight he was never likely to forget.

Blake was willing to guess that if that platform had taken them to the Gardener's Conservatory, it could probably go anywhere. After all, it was the Librarian's and he had no doubt that what-ever happened in any story, the Librarian knew all about it. Surely she could only know every-thing if she went to the actual worlds the writers created? He speculated that since the Librarian was not a writer herself, it was probably the case that platform travel was not restricted to authors only. He wasn't certain about this, but it seemed like a reasonable hypothesis.

As Blake related all of this to Colette in a quiet voice, the platform vibrated gently next to them, as if it had overheard his plan and was trembling with anticipation at the prospect of a trip outside the confines of the bookshelves.

'Now all we have to do is wait until Madame L's retired for the night, get the platform out of here, and into her office,' said Blake. 'Then we roll back the carpet, open the trapdoor and … you're on your way.'

'I don't like it,' whispered Colette. 'For a plan of great importance it lacks rigorous research. Perhaps this platform is the special vehicle of the Librarian, and in anyone else's hands it will go zipping who knows where? And what if it happens again that I go flying towards the world of Vivienne Small and crash right into the sky and slide like a soap bubble down glass? Only this time I don't land anywhere, I just keep falling.

And die. No, no, no. Not before I have found Tuesday. I think I will take my chances talking to this Librarian first.'

Blake was beginning to protest when the dimmed lights in the book room flickered and flared into full candescence. Blake and Colette heard the doors to the book room opening, then muffled footsteps hurrying across the floor.

'Behind here!' hissed Blake, pulling Colette into the gap between two towering ranks of bookshelves.

An imperious voice rang out. 'Who's there? Who *is* that? That had better not be you, Mr Luckhurst. Come out! Now!'

Colette withdrew into the shadows, but was astonished to see Blake step forwards into the light, tamed and cowed.

'Hi, Madame L. I'm … um …'

'Oh, my giddy aunt. It *is* you! Honestly, Blake Luckhurst. I do tire of your shenanigans. Truly, I do. Your book was due to be finished three months ago, and I will not tolerate any further delays! I do not care if Mr Bonner's incendiary device left him with serious facial injuries.

Write him a jolly good plastic surgeon and get on with it! He's an action hero, made of stern stuff. Quick healer.'

Colette stepped out from behind the bookshelf. In her great, furry black coat, she loomed over the tiny, silver-haired woman in the satin dressing-gown.

'If you will pardon me, Madame Lib—' Colette began, quite politely.

The Librarian turned a withering gaze on Colette, though it had to travel quite a distance upwards to reach the taller woman.

'Hush! Did I speak to you? I'll come to you momentarily.'

And Colette was astonished to find that there was, indeed, something in that voice that made her feel most unusually obedient. Colette did not, as a rule, do obedience.

'Off with you, Mr Luckhurst! What do you need? Pen, paper? There's some in the bureau in the foyer. Or is it food? Get something from the dining room and then get going. And here … don't ever say I don't do anything for you!'

191

The Librarian reached into the pocket of her dressing-gown and drew out a large, gold coin.

'Be very specific about where you want to go. No procrastinating. No additional characters that do not add to the plot. Get into the thick of it, Blake,' she said, pointing towards the book room's doors. 'Right this instant!'

Blake – head down and with no trace of his former confidence or magnanimity – made his way out of the huge room. At the door, he paused and glanced back.

'Um, Colette. Sorry ... tried,' he said. 'Later.'

And then he was gone.

'And *you*. If I am not mistaken, you are no writer,' said the Librarian to Colette. 'Into my office, now!'

'Sit down,' said the Librarian imperiously, resuming her seat on the chaise longue and gesturing to an elegant curved-back chair in the middle of the room. Colette sat.

'Thank you,' said Colette. 'I do apologise ...'

The Librarian interrupted. 'I require to know

who you are, and how you have managed to find your way into my Library.'

Colette did her best to smile a charming smile. As she looked perfectly enormous in her bearskin coat perched on the Librarian's delicate chair, this did not quite have the effect she desired.

'I am godmother to Tuesday McGillycuddy, who is in great danger, or so I am told by her dog, Baxterr. Baxterr himself has gone in search of Tuesday, but has not returned. Mr Luckhurst and I met by chance. It is clear, of course, that you are a person of great power here, and I must apply to you for assistance. I have promised her mother, you see. And I am a woman of my word. You know her mother, of course. I believe she is also here, somewhere, safe and well. I would not like to disturb Serendipity, at this present, delicate time, with bad news. I would simply like to have Tuesday returned to Brown Street so that when her mother returns all is well.'

'Bad news!' the Librarian said with a snort. 'Bad news? Tuesday is writing a story. Her mother should be proud, delighted! At least one of them is writing. That's all I can say.'

Colette drew herself very upright in her chair.

'It is true I am not an expert, but the green thread … I believe it is of concern.'

The Librarian smiled broadly and picked up her knitting and resumed her handiwork.

'Oh, Tuesday McGillycuddy is a very original young lady,' she said. 'I expect she's imagined something entirely new. Every now and then you get a writer that can do that, you know. I've had my eye on Ms McGillycuddy. I knew from the start that she was quite special.'

'I wish, nevertheless, to go into the world to ensure she is safe and well,' said Colette, still attempting to be charming.

'You know, this is not the first time I've been through this with friends and relatives of Ms McGillycuddy. For no good reason. Has anything terrible thus far befallen her? No! It has not! She is probably out there, right now, writing the book that will forge her career, and you want to check if she's *safe*. Heavens. Stories are not *safe*.'

'That is precisely my point,' said Colette drily. 'I have told you that I am a woman of my word and this means I will go to the world.'

The Librarian laughed loudly.

'Impossible!' she cried. 'My only concern is how best to get you home and out of here, where you do not belong. I hope I can rely upon your absolute discretion? This place has remained the closely guarded secret of writers for all time.'

Colette sighed. And had the Librarian known Colette a little better, she would have recognised the sigh as a warning. Quite calmly, Colette stood up, took two confident steps towards the Librarian, caught up the wool in the Librarian's hands, and tied it swiftly around the Librarian's upper body.

'Stop! Stop! Release me! You brute!' the Librarian squeaked, outraged. But Colette simply popped the remains of the ball of wool into the Librarian's mouth, silencing her. Then, quite methodically, she drew out some new skeins from the Librarian's knitting basket and proceeded to bind the small woman's equally small hands and legs. Before long, the Librarian was neatly trussed in a haze of fluffy purple wool. She stared in fury at Colette. Her pearl earrings were quivering, as if emanating rage.

'Wait there,' Colette said, then chuckled.

Colette visited the dining room and returned with a sarsaparilla spider, which she set down on the table beside the Librarian's chaise longue. She bent the red-and-white-striped straw and put it into the glass. But seeing that it was too low for the Librarian to comfortably reach, Colette grabbed a few books from the Librarian's private shelves to raise the glass up a little.

'We needn't be uncivil about this,' Colette said, removing the woolly stopper from the Librarian's mouth and waggling it in front of the Librarian. 'If you make a noise, or say a single word, I will have to replace my little cork. Now, with a simple nod of your head – yes or no – will the platform in the book room take me wherever I want to go?'

'How dare you!' said Madame Librarian.

Colette waggled the ball of wool at the Librarian.

'Not a word, I said. Nod yes or no.'

Madam Librarian stared at Colette in mute cold rage, not moving a muscle.

'Well,' said Colette. 'I see that you are not a person easily intimidated. I admire that. But it leaves me with only one option. I'm not particularly happy about it, but I find I must try out your platform.'

The Librarian glared at her as Colette rolled back the study's shimmery mauve carpet to reveal, as Blake had described, a trapdoor with a brass ringbolt for a handle.

Chapter Twenty

'Perfect. That's perfect. A brilliant story!' cried Loddon.

He sat up from where he had been lolling on the paper grass and clapped loudly.

In this story, Tuesday had sent Loddon in search of a giant who was throwing boulders onto a town. He had made friends with the giant, saving the town from certain disaster. Having received the appropriate accolades, including a lifetime supply of gold, he had decided to go with the giant to visit other places, riding high on his shoulders. The first town was saved – but perhaps other towns wouldn't be. Unless they paid.

Tuesday had discovered that Loddon much preferred stories in which he was the valiant hero who saved the town from the dragon, but was given the finest castle for doing so. Or he saved the city from a plague of cats, but when the townspeople refused to pay him, lured all the children away with his flute into the mountain and they were never seen again. He was a hero – of sorts. He never did anything for nothing.

'And now … another one,' Loddon said.

Tuesday groaned.

'Come on, Writer. We're having such fun. More! More!'

Tuesday looked around the confines of the paper cavern and then closed her eyes in despair. She was exhausted, her throat was hoarse, she was hungry, and the last thing in the world that she wanted to do was to tell another story to Loddon, about Loddon.

How long had she been here? Tuesday couldn't tell. Several times, she had returned to her cave exhausted, and slept. Several times Loddon had woken her by shouting, 'Story time!' in a loud and cheerful voice at the mouth of her cave, then demanded she come down to the tree and tell stories. For hours and hours. When she came down the stairs the paper sun was out, but as soon as she returned to her cave, the moon and stars appeared. Whether these were real days or nights outside in the world of Vivienne Small, Tuesday had no way of knowing.

The last of her supply of nuts was gone. All that remained were two slices of dried apple. Her stomach felt as empty as a peanut shell. It felt like days since Tuesday had watched Ermengarde nibble on the final meagre offerings of two cashews. She wondered if they were both going to slowly starve to death.

Tuesday's dreams had been weird, full of cream buns and chocolate-iced doughnuts, deep-fried sausages and jugs of cola. These were not even foods she liked, but for some reason her mind kept suggesting them.

Tuesday had given much thought to escaping while Loddon was asleep. She imagined making her way with Ermengarde out through the tunnel that had brought them here. But she knew that if she made it back to the outside world, they wouldn't survive for long, not without shelter from the snow and the terrible winter. Besides, as soon as Loddon woke, he'd be after her. She couldn't sail *Storm Rider* and she had no other means of escape. But if she left it even one more day, she wasn't going to have the energy to go anywhere. Already, though she was sure she had only been awake for a few hours, she wanted to sleep again. She was tired, dizzy and her mouth was dry. The water that was seeping down the wall of her cave helped, but she wanted to drink buckets of water.

Tuesday and Ermengarde had explored the tunnel leading away from her cave, Tuesday tracking their wanderings using the small knife from Colette's poncho. She had made arrows at various tunnel openings, but the dusky light in the tunnels did not make it easy to find the way back. Also the tunnels had a bad habit of coming out at the edge of the cavern with huge gaps between her and the nearest staircase.

The tunnels and caves were quite fascinating in themselves. In some she found the walls still covered in pages from notebooks and sketches. She recognised her mother's handwriting. She wondered, at first, how it was possible that she had been able to go so deep into her mother's world. But she didn't have to explore very far to understand. Here and there she found her own drawings and stories. One picture that had been rather savagely torn in half was one of Tuesday's pictures of Vivienne Small. She remembered the day she had drawn it her mother had said, 'Oh, I didn't know Vivienne had blue wings.'

'Didn't you?' said Tuesday. 'Oh, yes.'

'But she's not a fairy,' Serendipity had said.

'No, she just has wings.'

'She's too fierce to be a fairy,' said Serendipity.

And they had laughed, because Tuesday had been going through a fierce stage herself.

Tuesday missed her mother intensely each time she looked at the fragments of words and pictures on the walls. She wondered where her mother was. Was she already back at Brown Street, or somewhere in this world? Or another world entirely?

'Come *on*, Writer,' Loddon said, his voice breaking into Tuesday's hazy thoughts. 'Another story! More! More!'

Loddon threw himself down on the grass and folded his hands behind his head. He closed his eyes.

'Loddon, there can be no more story time until I have something to eat.'

Loddon opened his eyes and stared at her in disbelief.

'Nonsense! Writers don't need food. Writers need words!'

'Loddon, I'm not going to be able to get down the stairs tomorrow – or even up again later, if you don't get me some food,' Tuesday said. 'Seriously, I could starve.'

'Oooooh,' said Loddon. 'Oh, yes, I know how that feels. You left me alone and I was starving too. I had no stories.'

Loddon quickly plucked at some grass, ripping the paper shreds and holding them out to Tuesday.

'Food?' he said. 'Then story?'

'That is not actually food,' Tuesday said.

'Don't tell me you're hungry if you won't eat what I give you.'

'This isn't food,' Tuesday repeated, tearing a wad of paper grass and waving it back at him. 'If there *isn't* any food here, then we'll have to leave. You'll have to take me back, you understand.'

'Back?' asked Loddon. 'Back where?'

'To the ship,' Tuesday said, pointing towards the tunnel. 'So we can sail for food.'

'Out of the question. Now you're here you're not allowed to go. Not ever.'

Tuesday thought for a moment, then said, 'Loddon, where do you go – when it's night here?'

'My room,' said Loddon.

'Would you like to show me your room?' Tuesday asked.

'Maybe,' said Loddon.

Tuesday expected it to be up some frightening staircase, but it wasn't.

Loddon walked around the trunk of the tree, then looked back thoughtfully at Tuesday. After a long moment, he beckoned to her. To Tuesday's amazement, Loddon reached for a large ring in the ground at the foot of the tree and pulled up a trapdoor that was covered with paper grass. Inside there was a ladder. Down Tuesday went, following Loddon, into a room panelled with what appeared to be tin. Loddon's green glow brightened, giving the room an eerie sombre light.

'Isn't it wonderful?' he asked. 'You gave it to me. You told me I'd be safe here and you'd always tell me stories.'

Tuesday knocked on the walls and it made a dull metal sound. She looked up. The roof was tin too. And then she realised where she was.

The boy called Loddon, underneath the tree,
Can you hear him when he calls to me?
I put him in a box far down below,
He's down where all the stories go.

She was in Loddon's box. She shivered. She was down where all the stories go. How was she going to get herself out of this predicament? Her stomach growled and she felt faint.

'Loddon?' Tuesday whispered.

'Yes, Writer?' Loddon said. Down here in his box, seated on the shredded paper that covered the floor, he looked like a child sitting on a mat in a kindergarten.

'I need you to go and get me some food. You might need to take *Storm Rider*. I'm going to need lots of food if you want me to keep telling you stories. And water. I need fresh water. It won't take you long. If you leave now, you might be back by tomorrow morning.'

Loddon frowned. 'Are you sure about this food thing? Or is it a tricky writer's trick?'

'People die without food and water, Loddon. I will die.'

Loddon thought for a moment, and then climbed a few rungs of the ladder.

'All right, Writer. I will get this food for you,' he said, gesturing magnanimously. 'And I will take my new friend the giant with me! But you can stay here!'

Tuesday cried out, but it was too late. Everything went black as Loddon leapt up the ladder and slammed the trapdoor. She banged on it. She pushed against it. But it wouldn't budge. Tuesday sank to the floor and thought she might cry. The paper world above had been hard enough, but to be stuck in this pitch-black box was almost unbearable. What if he didn't come back?

Tuesday reached up to pat Ermengarde, nestled in her hood, but Ermengarde was not there.

'Ermengarde!' she called. 'Ermengarde?'

But there was no familiar scuttling noise, no small warm body clambering up her arm. Tuesday felt about the floor in the darkness. Where had Ermengarde gone? And then she thought of the saying that rats always desert a sinking ship. Was she a sinking ship? What if she was stuck here forever? How would anyone ever find her?

Chapter Twenty-one

Wandering beyond the boatshed, Serendipity again found the overgrown garden of her childhood home. She could hear her parents shouting at one another in the house, and she had no desire to see that up close. She had so many memories of days like that where the fights went on for hours. So she made her way to the pear tree and realised there was a small girl lying in the grass.

'Hello,' said the girl.

A thrill went through Serendipity as the girl raised her head and smiled. Serendipity had no photos of herself as a child, but she recognised this girl straight away. Partly because she looked like a version of Tuesday at six or seven. But mostly because you always recognise yourself if you come across yourself, even in an unexpected moment.

'Hello, Sarah,' said Serendipity. 'What are you doing?'

'Watching clouds,' said the small Sarah. 'Do you want to play a game?'

Serendipity lay down beside her in the grass and stared up at the clouds too.

'All right,' she said.

'Okay. So, we ask each other questions,' said Sarah. 'Do you want to go first?'

'What's your favourite colour?' asked Serendipity.

'Blue. But in this game, you can't just say a colour, you have to say the special way the colour works,' said Sarah. 'So my answer is blue. The sort of blue the sky is now, when I'm under my favourite tree and the whole afternoon is shining.'

Serendipity nodded.

'My turn,' said Sarah. 'What's your favourite thing to wear?'

'Boots,' said Serendipity. 'Black lace-up boots that will walk me anywhere and never wear out. What about you? What's *your* favourite thing to wear?'

'You can't ask me the same question I asked you, otherwise it gets boring,' said Sarah. 'But because you haven't played before, I'll tell you. An umbrella. I know it's not officially clothing, but they're fun. And they can be fierce.'

Serendipity smiled and nodded.

'What's your favourite thing to do?' asked Sarah.

'I like writing in the morning before breakfast when the whole house is quiet,' said Serendipity.

'I like writing,' said Sarah. 'It's my favourite thing to do, too.'

'Don't stop,' said Serendipity. Then she asked, 'What's your favourite noise?'

'The sound of the breeze arriving in the garden when it's been hot and still. The leaves always seem pleased to rustle around in it,' said Sarah. 'What's your favourite smell?'

'Oh,' said Serendipity, 'that would be the

smell of my husband's blueberry pancakes on a Sunday morning.'

'I've never had pancakes,' said Sarah.

'You will,' said Serendipity.

And so they went on as bright clouds gathered and dispersed, and the world made steady progress past the sun.

'What's your favourite idea?' asked Serendipity.

'That's a hard one,' said Sarah. She thought about this as she chewed a long piece of grass, and then she said, 'I think it's that there are other worlds where people are living and one day I'll meet them.'

She seemed to dwell on this thought for a few moments and then asked Serendipity, 'What's your favourite word?'

'Imagine,' said Serendipity.

'I like "imagine" too. You can ride anywhere on "imagine",' said Sarah. Then she added, 'Loddon likes "imagine" too.'

'Who?'

'Loddon. I tell him all my stories. He's safe now.'

'Safe?' asked Serendipity.

The girl was quiet for a little while. 'He kept climbing in the window and waking me up. Once he tried to tie me up and drag me back to this tree. And once he tried to set fire to all my notebooks. So I gave him my pencil box from school.'

'And you put him in it?'

'Yes, how did you know?'

Serendipity shrugged.

'He's all right,' Sarah continued. 'I tell him stories. If I don't he gets hungry. But he mustn't get out.'

'Because he's mean?'

Sarah nodded. 'Mean is my least favourite thing.'

Without time seeming to pass, the shadows had grown long across the garden. Sarah jumped up.

'I'd better go in,' she said.

Serendipity took the notebook she had carried from the boatshed out of her pocket and handed it to Sarah.

'Thank you!' said Sarah. 'I'm always running out of paper.'

'I remember,' said Serendipity.

'Will you come back?' asked Sarah.

'Maybe. Or you might come forward,' said Serendipity.

'That's a good idea,' said Sarah. 'I'll see you then.'

As Sarah ran towards the house, Serendipity had to stifle an urge to chase after her. But even as Sarah ran, she became hazy, indistinct, like a mirage. And then she vanished altogether. So too did the shabby white house. Then Serendipity was standing on a vacant city block. The ground was covered in gravel and weeds and the block was hemmed in by a paling fence that was marked, here and there, with bright splashes of graffiti.

Parked on the vacant block was a food van. There was a delicious smell in the air, and someone in the van was cooking. Serendipity moved closer.

'Hello?' she said.

The cook turned and as he did so, Serendipity lost the sense of solid ground beneath her feet.

'Denis?'

He smiled at her, and something inside Serendipity broke. She felt as if whatever had been torn apart inside her when Denis died was breaking open again. The world beneath her shook and shattered, but he was reaching for her, and pulling her to safety.

Chapter Twenty-two

With Vivienne astride his shoulders, her wings injured and her body bruised, Baxterr flew, and flew, and flew. Seeming never to tire, he crossed the vast width of the Restless Sea from shore to shore, backwards and forwards, his nose searching on the breeze for any scent of Tuesday, his eyes combing the water for a glimpse of her, or any sign of the ship that Vivienne had described. Snow flurried around them, and a biting wing blew, laced with shards of ice. But still Baxterr searched.

Every now and then, he would let out a small bark or whimper, and fly lower to investigate something he had seen – or thought he had seen – among the endless waves. But it was usually just a derry bird, perched blithely upon the wild water, or else the rising flukes of a neverwhale. Mostly, though, it was only a shadow of his hopes and wishful thoughts.

From her place on Baxterr's shoulders, Vivienne could see the world spread beneath her like a watery map, obscured from time to time by low fog. Dotted here and there were islands edged with cliffs, frozen white and black. As Baxterr flew west, she watched the snow-bound Mountains of Margalov rise up on the horizon, and realised, with a pang, just how long it had been since she had seen their lower slopes in their proper shades of purple, blue and forest green. All the land in sight was wintering and starving. She shuddered and her teeth chattered, but not only from the cold, and she burrowed deep into Baxterr's fur, doing all she could to stay warm against the chill that was rippling through her from her injured wings. Her head throbbed and her thoughts swam, and although she was loath to admit it, she knew the wounds Loddon had inflicted were becoming infected.

'Arroooo,' howled Baxterr, and dived seawards.

Vivienne felt his ears and his spirits lift, and then droop as he realised that what he had seen was just another derry bird riding a wave, its spiky crest fluttering in the sharp breeze. Baxterr skimmed the waves, and then began to climb into the sky to continue his search.

As the day wore on, they found themselves approaching the southern shore of the Restless Sea, a remote and mostly uninhabited part of Vivienne Small's world. The coastline was a series of high ragged cliffs, but Vivienne had rarely found any particular reason to scale them. Inland from the cliffs the coastal land with its small, thorny shrubs gave way gradually to sand. Here lay a wide, forbidding desert that in the past had glowed vividly with heat. Vivienne remembered several savage nights she had spent in that desert. She remembered the days of desperate thirst, grit blinding her eyes, death haunting every breath. She had hoped never to come here again.

Vivienne squinted down at that remote land-scape. The Purple Desert no longer reflected its name. It was grey with cold and ice. But ripping across it, as if it had been hacked through with a badly wielded axe, was a vast rupture in the land. The world had split its very fabric in two, leaving a mark as far as her eye could see. She remembered well the earthquake that had shaken the forest, unsettled the sea and caused rocks to tumble and birds to cry strange songs for days afterwards. It had marked the coming of the deep and endless winter. Here in front of her was the epicentre of the great quake. But at the place where the rupture met the sea … what was *that*?

'Doggo, look!' Vivienne called, over the wind. 'Over there in the shadow of that landslide. Is that a mast?'

Baxterr changed course and made directly for the shape in the distance.

The ship was aground. The yawning gap created by the earthquake opened behind it, dark and forbidding. The ship's sails hung limply in wintry light.

Baxterr glided in and landed on the frozen shore. Vivienne slipped from his back and listened. Baxterr whined.

'I know, doggo,' Vivienne whispered. 'This is the ship. She might still be here.'

Instinctively she spread her wings, planning to fly up onto the deck of *Storm Rider* and investigate. Too late, she remembered her stitched wings. The pain of trying to unfurl them was unbearable, and a wave of dizziness washed over her, scrambling her thoughts. She sat on the icy shore and breathed deeply, one hand seeking the reassurance of Baxterr's warm fur.

Then Baxterr's ears pricked up, and Vivienne heard it, too. It was a muffled voice, the grass-boy's voice, coming from below decks on *Storm Rider*.

'It's *him*,' Vivienne whispered to Baxterr. 'Let me onto the ship, quietly.'

Cautiously, Vivienne scrambled up and Baxterr lifted his huge head over the deck railing, so she could tiptoe over the back of his head and down his snout onto the deck. With careful footsteps, Vivienne edged along the railing in the direction of a companionway that led to the ship's fo'c'sle, forward cabins and galley. No sooner had she reached it when an object came flying out of the opening, right past her. It was the sole of a shoe. It landed on the deck with a flap, alongside a strange collection of other objects. There were some candles, a box of fishhooks, and a rather large neverwhale bone.

'Eat, eat, eat. What does she want to eat for?' Loddon was muttering to himself. 'Can she eat this? Maybe. Here goes.'

And with that, he threw a tin of brass cleaner up onto the deck.

Silently, Vivienne climbed onto the low roof above the companionway. She had to breathe deeply and move slowly because every movement of her wings caused her vision to go a little wavery. Where was Tuesday? She peered up into the rigging, wondering if Ermengarde was still there, somewhere amid the spars and sails. But she could see no scurrying shape, hear no scuttling feet.

'Da dee dum di naaa, hnnaaa, na,' Loddon hummed. And then, half singing and half humming, 'Well, giant, what would you eat if this was you? Whole cities, I expect. Ho, na na ni dum de dum, crunch crunch crunch, tear the doors of houses, chew the chimneys bare …'

Vivienne cast around for a weapon of some kind. There had to be something … it was the perfect opportunity to take him by surprise, now, while he was below decks and unawares.

'Stove in the windows, break the balconies …'

The off-key voice was getting louder. Vivienne realised the grassboy was coming up the companionway. She pressed herself flat on the varnished timber, keeping out of sight. She tried to get Baxterr's attention, wanting to tell him to stay below the deck railing, but he was busily sniffing at the sand beyond the prow of *Storm Rider*, having picked up a scent trail that led deeper into the crevasse.

'Ho, ho!' cried the boy, on deck by now. 'What are you? A giant dog? No, that's wrong! My writer promised me a giant, not a giant dog. Go away and come back when you're a giant!'

And with that, Loddon picked up the never-whale bone from the deck and threw it viciously at Baxterr. Baxterr rounded on Loddon, growling more ferociously than Vivienne Small had imagined possible. The growl echoed around the bay, filling the frozen space with menace. As Baxterr approached Loddon, his lips were curled back, top and bottom, and his white teeth gleamed in the darkness.

While Loddon laughed and scrabbled about for something else to throw at Baxterr, Vivienne slipped through the companionway roof and hurried below deck. She searched the galley for Tuesday, but there was no one there. She searched for knives, but found none of those either. She hurried through the saloon, searching for a weapon of any kind. And there it was, resting on hooks high on the wall. A crossbow, and a quiver of steel-tipped bolts. Vivienne reached up and brought down the crossbow. Compared with her light, timber recurve bow, this was a monstrous thing that required most of her strength merely to hold it. Her shoulders groaning with the weight, her body straining against the pain in her wings, she slid the quiver of bolts over her shoulder, selected one, and fitted it to the crossbow.

Step by step, Vivienne Small made her way up the companionway and onto the deck, where Loddon stood at the very prow of the ship taunting a snarling Baxterr. She lifted the crossbow and got the green boy squarely in her sights.

'Where is Tuesday?' Vivienne demanded.

'Not telling,' Loddon said.

Enraged, she loosed the bolt. It flew, fast and true, spearing a hole in Loddon's grass shirt sleeve and pinning him to the ship's railing.

'That wasn't very nice, Vivienne Small,' Loddon cried out in a furious, petulant voice, ripping himself free.

But Vivienne only fitted another bolt to the crossbow and moved towards him.

'Where is she?' she asked.

'One, two, three, four, five, once I caught a girl alive,' he sang. 'Six, seven, eight, nine, ten, I'll never let her go again. You'll never find her.'

Loddon glanced at the cliff beyond the boat where the chasm began.

'She's down *there*?' Vivienne asked.

Baxterr snarled.

'Take me to her,' said Vivienne Small.

'I don't think so,' Loddon said.

Vivienne stepped closer, and aimed the bolt right between his eyes.

He laughed. 'Do you think I'm afraid of that little toy?' And with that Loddon shrugged out of his torn shirt and, with his two hands, drew the strands of his woven body apart.

Vivienne saw he was entirely made of bright springtime grass.

Loddon reached up, buried his hands in hair and tore himself in half, from head to toe. The left side of him swept around one side of her, while the right side of him twirled around the other.

Vivienne was alarmed to see a little black shape drop from one half of Loddon and run across the deck towards her.

'Ermengarde!' she cried, but there was no time to collect up her little friend.

Vivienne spun around to see the two halves of Loddon meeting up and recombining, rather as if he were being zippered back together. She was aware of Baxterr barking in fury.

'Rat!' Loddon yelled. 'Revolting creature.'

He leapt towards Ermengarde, slamming a foot down on the deck, trying to crush her.

Vivienne couldn't bear it — she threw down the crossbow and hurled her own body over the top of Ermengarde's scuttling black form. She was just in time. Loddon's foot crashed beside Vivienne's face.

'I don't think you're going to be needing *these* anymore, do you?' Loddon said, scooping up the quiver of crossbow bolts at Vivienne's side, and retrieving the crossbow from the deck. He loaded it and pointed it at Baxterr.

'No,' Vivienne yelled. 'No! Baxterr, get out of the way!'

Baxterr took flight. Loddon loosed a bolt.

Baxterr rolled sideways, then howled. The bolt had grazed his wing, sending shreds of loose fur flying into the sky.

Vivienne yelled, 'Fly, Baxterr, fly!'

Baxterr flew up, then spun around and hovered above the ship. Loddon casually loaded another bolt and fired.

This one took Baxterr in his front leg. He howled and twisted away, soaring into the sky.

'Dum dum de dum,' Loddon hummed, watching and waiting for a third shot at Baxterr.

'Ermengarde, my wings,' Vivienne whispered.

With that, Ermengarde scampered out from underneath Vivienne's hair and began to nibble. One two, three, four, five, six stitches …

'Eenie, meenie, miney, mo. Catch a doggie by the toe. If he hollers … shoot him again!' cried Loddon, but this time, his shot missed.

Nine, ten, eleven, twelve stitches …

Loddon reloaded and Baxterr wheeled away once more. Vivienne could see blood on his great foot and at the edge of his wing.

Fifteen stitches, sixteen, seventeen …

Loddon was prancing about the deck with the crossbow sight to his face. Each time Baxterr lunged, Loddon laughed and feinted.

'I'll get you in the head in a minute, and then D … E … D … spells out you go,' Loddon sang.

Vivienne felt the last stitch come undone. She could see that Loddon had Baxterr in his sight.

'Hold tight, Ermengarde,' she whispered.

Just as Loddon fired, Vivienne spread her wings and leapt onto Loddon.

The bolt missed Baxterr, for it had shredded the flesh on Vivienne's shoulder. She reeled with agony and dropped to the deck. Trying to regain her feet, she was straightaway knocked over by a force that, at first, she did not understand. She heard rumbling and cracking. Sections of cliff were breaking away and smashing around *Storm Rider*. Rocks fell on the deck and others broke masts and rigging.

'Yes!' roared Loddon in triumph. 'It's my giant! He's come! He's walking over the earth right now, Vivienne Small. I will feed you to him for his breakfast and I will give him that dog as a pet. My friend the giant will make that dog do as he's told.'

'You're delusional,' Vivienne gasped.

From where she clung to the deck, Vivienne could see the split in the earth widening beyond the ship. And then the air above her was full of golden brown fur. It was Baxterr, his eyes rolling with fear from the thunderous sounds all around. With all her courage, and in defiance of her pain, Vivienne sprang into the air landing awkwardly on Baxterr's shoulders. Rocks continued to fall as the cliffs and shore crumbled, then Baxterr swept them upwards on a gust of bitterly cold wind. Vivienne could see Loddon standing tall and green on the deck of *Storm Rider*. He held his arms to the sky as the crevasse that had once ended at the broken cliffs tore its way into the sea.

'Nothing can hurt me!' Loddon roared.

But then the sea poured in and filled the split in the earth, turning it into a swirling morass of mud and rock and water. *Storm Rider* began spinning like a boat above a plughole, round and round and round. And then, with a fearful sucking noise, it was dragged down into the swirling flood, and was gone. The earth stilled. The rocks that were falling from the cliffs came to rest.

'Tuesday,' Vivienne Small whispered.

Baxterr flew low along the widening fracture as it deepened inland. It was sinking, section by section. Rock and earth were pouring, unstoppably, down into the abyss.

Baxterr flew the full long length of the split to where at last it ended in the icy sands of the Purple Desert. They came to ground, and Vivienne slid down from Baxterr's shoulders. For a moment,

Baxterr sat on his haunches staring disbelievingly at the crater of earth and the fracture leading away, back to the sea so far beyond. Vivienne placed a hand gently above his colossal, wounded paw. She felt his sorrow echo painfully through the rips in her wings.

Under the wintry sky, Baxterr the Winged Dog threw back his great head and began to howl. It was a howl of utter despair and it rang out, loud and deep and terrible, across the world of Vivienne Small. It reverberated through the skies and echoed deep into the mountains and forests. In the whole of the world, there was not a single creature that did not hear Baxterr's cry, nor any who could keep from shuddering at the chilling, desperate sound of it.

Chapter Twenty-three

Tuesday, too, felt the earth shake. Inside Loddon's box, she braced herself, hands gripping the shredded paper. Was this Loddon returning? Or something worse? Tuesday scrambled across the floor in what she thought was the direction of the trapdoor, but the box was shuddering and swaying. She fell heavily against a side wall, bruising her shoulder and hip. It was as if the earth around the box had become liquid and the box was washing about in it.

'Help!' Tuesday called. 'Help me!'

She scrabbled at the walls, listening to the thundering crashes beyond. She covered her head, heart thudding like a jackhammer.

I'm in a nightmare, Tuesday thought.

Tuesday had been prone to recurring night-
mares when she was younger. The worst one was
when she dreamed of Baxterr being stolen by a
trio of witches who blindfolded him so he could
never find his way home.

Tuesday had always been grateful that she
didn't have the kind of parents who turned on
the light for just a minute and then said, 'It's only
a dream, now go back to sleep.' To deal with
the problem of witches, Serendipity had brought
home some Witch Repellent. It was a special
formula that came in a handy spray pack, was
bright yellow and smelled of peppermint essence.
The label had looked suspiciously handmade and
bore the words, *Spray your pet twice every Sunday
as required*, which, for a long time, Tuesday had
done. Baxterr had been unconvinced by this
ritual, but Tuesday had found it immensely
reassuring.

Denis had always been the type of father who,
when required in the night, would sit beside
Tuesday until she managed to find her way back
to a peaceful sleep. And he had always reassured

her that, should the Witch Repellent fail for any reason, Baxterr would find his way home even if he were blind and deaf, because he would be able to smell Tuesday and that would be enough.

'Please find me soon,' Tuesday whispered.

The box continued to shiver and shake as the earth beyond it heaved and finally settled. Tuesday imagined her mother holding her, and her father sitting beside her, and Baxterr flying blindfolded all the way to find her, even though she was so far from home.

Chapter Twenty-four

Serendipity sat bolt upright, her heart hammering so hard that it felt as if it would bruise itself against her ribs. Inside her mind, the last pictures of her dream lingered — the earth falling away beneath her feet, and Denis pulling her to safety. It had felt terrifyingly real, but it was all slipping away now, like water over sand. She realised she was in the boatshed, and it was dark outside. She was quite safe. There was no earthquake. But still something felt wrong.

Serendipity threw back the counterpane, leapt out of bed and looked out at the lake. It was utterly still and stars seemed to hover just below the surface of the silky, black water. Definitely no earthquake here. Then came a sound that turned Serendipity's blood to ice. *Aroooo … arooooo … arooooo …*

It was a dog, howling as though its heart was breaking. But, Serendipity realised, it wasn't just any dog.

'Baxterr?' she whispered. Although she had never heard him howl in such a desperate way, she would have known the particular tone of his voice anywhere. And if Baxterr was howling, then where was Tuesday? What had happened to her? Why wasn't she at home? Weren't they all at home, Baxterr, Tuesday and Colette? Baxterr would only howl like that if something dreadful had happened to the person he loved the most.

Wild and terrible thoughts filled Serendipity's head. She threw a woollen wrap over the top of her white pyjamas, then she searched about for her boots. She jammed them on and dashed out of the boatshed and into the moonlit night. With determined steps, she hurried up the pathway in the direction of the Library.

Serendipity didn't pause to admire how lovely the gardens were at night, or to observe the beautiful patterns of the surrounding mist, or to see what was on offer at the dining room buffet. She didn't even consider stepping into the great book room to gaze on the immense wonder of all the stories of the world collected in a single room. She strode purposefully towards the door of the Librarian's study and flung it open.

'And about time, too!' shrieked the Librarian, who – in her attempts to get free from her cocoon of mauve knitting yarn – had toppled over sideways on her chaise longue. 'I was beginning to think that I was going to languish here all night! Where, I ask you, are the writers who keep at it until dawn? Hmm? I have been calling and calling, and nobody has come to my aid. What is the world coming to, I ask you?'

Serendipity took in the extraordinary sight of the Librarian. Her silver hair was sticking out erratically and her eyes were dark purple with rage. Serendipity could see that a drink of some sort had been spilled over the mauve damask fabric of the chaise. On the floor were puddles of milky liquid, and a red-and-white drinking straw. The carpet that usually covered the floor was rolled up to one side of the room. In the middle of the polished floorboards there was a trapdoor, flung wide open. She could feel a faint current of cool air drifting into the room, as if from a window left open on a summer's evening.

Tiptoeing to the edge of the opening, Serendipity was momentarily awed by the spellbinding sight of millions of worlds orbiting in space.

'Set me upright, for goodness' sake!' the Librarian bellowed. 'And untie me, this instant!'

Serendipity rushed to the Librarian's side and hefted her back up into a sitting position. The Librarian let out a noise that made Serendipity think of an insulted chicken.

'What happened?' Serendipity asked. 'Who tied you up?'

'Totally undignified,' the Librarian moaned. 'Get me free! Get me free!'

'I'm working on it,' Serendipity said. 'It would help if you sat still.'

After searching for a moment, Serendipity located scissors in a desk drawer and wielded them.

'Are you a fool?' said the Librarian. 'The wool will be useless. Unwrap me!'

Serendipity searched quickly for an end in the yarn and began to unwind it as swiftly as she could. Every so often there were skilfully tied knots that had kept the trussing tidy and effective, despite the Librarian's struggles.

'Madame Librarian, who *did* this? And why?'

'Well, you are not – as it turns out – innocent in this matter. Some enormous ursine friend of *yours*, it was.'

'Ursine?'

'Bear-like. Feline, canine, ovine, bovine, vulpine … of that word family, you know,' said the Librarian, who, even in her present state, found it hard to resist spouting a list of useful vocabulary.

'Bear-like?'

'Yes, yes. Bear-like. Get *on* with it, Serendipity.'

Serendipity racked her brain, trying to think of any writers she knew who resembled bears. Or, indeed, any writers that the Librarian might consider to be Serendipity's friends. But she drew a blank. Then came a thought that made her blood turn to ice.

'The bear-like person. Was her name Colette Baden-Baden?'

'I don't care what she's called. She has assaulted me and broken every sacred rule of this place.'

'Colette's not a writer!' Serendipity said, her voice shrill with alarm.

'You don't have to tell *me* that, my dear. It's obvious! She has stolen my platform and made off with it.'

Serendipity glanced at the trapdoor. She tried to imagine what it was that could make Colette so desperate that she would go out there into that sky full of worlds. Her heart pounded.

'Please tell me Tuesday was with her.'

'Tuesday? No, that woman — whatever you call her — was quite alone. She was trying to find Tuesday. Wanting to go to the world of Vivienne Small.'

'So that's where Tuesday's gone?' Serendipity said to the Librarian. 'That can't be so bad, can it?'

'Bad?' said the Librarian. 'Of course not. The girl's writing. Which is exactly what she should be doing.'

Then Serendipity remembered what had brought her running to the Library.

'I felt an earthquake, Madame Librarian. A big one. And I thought I heard Baxterr. He was howling. Something is terribly wrong. Is Tuesday *there*?'

'There was an earthquake of quite considerable magnitude when you lost your Denis. Plunged the world into a bitter winter. I've seen it happen before. It's the shock, you see. And if I'm not mistaken, there was an aftershock a short while ago. Quite natural, I would have thought. I'm anxious to see what Tuesday makes of all this. Could be quite thrilling, don't you think?'

Serendipity took the Librarian by her still-partly-tangled-up shoulders.

'But Tuesday, is she there? Why did Baxterr howl?'

'Heavens! How would I know? I've been here, imprisoned,' the Librarian spluttered. 'Now can you *please* concentrate on what you're doing?'

But Serendipity had dashed out the French doors of the Librarian's office and onto the balcony. The night was misty and warm and utterly tranquil, but Serendipity had eyes for nothing but the binoculars on the railings. She rushed to the nearest set, but could see only blackness, as if the lenses were capped.

'Oh, how could I forget?' she said.

As fast as she had run to the verandah, Serendipity ran back to the Librarian's study, where the small woman was still working her way free of her bindings.

'A coin, Madame Librarian,' Serendipity said, breathless. 'Quickly.'

But the Librarian only fixed her with a cool stare.

'You've a nerve,' she said.

'But it's my world. I need to get there. Right now,' Serendipity said, feeling stricken.

The Librarian turned back to untying herself.

'It took me by surprise, I have to say, when Tuesday first came here and found her way into your world. But find her way there she did, didn't she? I wasn't happy about that, as you know, but she proved herself worthy. So, I wonder, Serendipity – whose world is it right now? Yours? Or hers?'

'*Ours*,' Serendipity cried. 'It's both of ours. I need a coin, Madame Librarian. I have to go to her.'

'One writer at a time in a world, Serendipity. Rules are rules.'

'Please, Madame Librarian. You have to help me. You have to let me in.'

'I do not have to do anything of the sort.'

'You must!'

But the Librarian only narrowed her eyes.

'No, Ms Smith. I must not.'

Chapter Twenty-five

There is a particular texture to true blackness. It is like seeing the beginning of time, long before there were stars or worlds. Seeing that kind of blackness can make you feel very small and very alone.

Tuesday was lying on her back on the shredded paper. There was no sound other than her breathing. Her stomach had given up making pathetic attempts to gurgle because it had finally decided that there was absolutely nothing in it to digest, and all the gurgling in the world wasn't going to change that. She thought she had just woken up – but it was hard to tell because there was no difference between having her eyes closed and having her eyes open.

She had been having some strange conversations in the darkness. Maybe these had happened in her sleep, or maybe while she was awake. She had gone past being panicked and frightened, and being sad, and being deeply worried, and being terribly lonely, and being completely exhausted. She had banged and scratched and pushed against the trapdoor and the walls of the box, but to no effect. She had called and sung and recited poetry and even danced, because there was nothing else to do in the blackness.

But now she was feeling something else. She wasn't sure quite what, but if she'd had to name it, she might have said she was calm. Calm while knowing she was in a box, in the earth, at the bottom of a long tunnel carved by Loddon, who had lived in these catacombs for a very, very long time and who had eaten stories for food. Tuesday understood about stories feeling like food, but her body knew the difference. This was why she was lying down. She felt faint whenever she moved.

In this new state of calmness, Tuesday was having a conversation with her mother. She could see Serendipity sitting at her desk at Brown Street typing on her typewriter. Serendipity looked up and smiled as Tuesday approached, and moved back her chair. Tuesday sat on her lap and Serendipity put her arms around her. Even though Tuesday was getting quite big to be doing this, it still felt like a good thing to do. Her mother smelled of the city after rain.

'Mum, what's the collective noun for a flock of Winged Dogs?'

'A purpose,' Serendipity replied. 'Remember when I was writing *Vivienne Small and the Mountains of Margalov*? I said to you "a pack of Winged Dogs can't be a flock", and then we talked about other collective nouns. Like a murder of crows, and a misbelief of painters, a parliament of owls …'

'And a bloat of hippopotamuses,' said Tuesday.

'A clowder of cats, but a kindle of kittens.'

'A smack of jellyfish,' said Tuesday.

'Yes!' said Serendipity. 'And then you said: "a *purpose* of Winged Dogs".'

Tuesday leaned her cheek against her mother's hair.

'Mum?' Tuesday asked. 'What do I do now? I'm stuck in my story.'

Serendipity said, 'Sometimes the only thing to do is wait. You can't rush these things.'

'What if you're lost? And where you're lost is the darkest, most frightening moment that keeps going on forever and ever?'

'Just wait,' said Serendipity. 'The next thing will come. Writing takes a particular sort of courage. The sort of courage nobody understands unless they've been stuck in the dark with no way out. I know you have that.'

'Mum?' Tuesday whispered. 'What if waiting isn't working?'

'Maybe you need to switch to another scene. Is anything else happening in the book?' asked Serendipity.

'I hope so,' said Tuesday. 'I hope Baxterr has somehow found Vivienne Small and they are, at this very moment, coming to rescue me.'

'Or Colette,' suggested Serendipity.

'I wish Colette was here right now,' said Tuesday, 'ripping Loddon to pieces.'

'I didn't mean to invent someone who would cause such problems,' said Serendipity. 'He was my friend. He was my first friend. And he loved my stories.'

'If I really needed you, you would come, wouldn't you?' asked Tuesday.

'Of course,' said Serendipity.

'This is the worst place I have ever been and I'm not sure I'm ever going to get out. Even Ermengarde has abandoned me.'

'Just wait, darling,' Serendipity said. 'Right now there is nothing else for it.'

So Tuesday waited. She listened and waited and waited and listened. Nothing happened. She might have slept some more. She might have dreamed. She might have had other conversations. It was too dark and lonely to know. All she knew was that she was sick of being in this box. She was sick of being trapped and frightened. She wanted Loddon to come back and open the trapdoor. She wanted to get out of the paper cavern. She wanted to see Baxterr. She wanted to fly home. She wanted …

And then she heard the unmistakable sound of a match striking. A light swam nearby. Tuesday squinted at the unexpected brightness and sat up.

'Hello?' she said. 'Who's there?'

'Anyone for blueberry pancakes?' asked Denis McGillycuddy.

'Dad!' said Tuesday. 'Dad!'

She leapt up and flung herself into his arms. He wore a pink-and-white striped shirt under a white apron and he looked just as she remembered him best.

'You came!' said Tuesday.

'Of course,' said Denis. 'Things were getting desperate.'

Tuesday observed a lantern-lit table set for two, with candles and plates and cutlery. On a large platter was a steaming stack of blueberry pancakes, a jug of maple syrup and a bowl of vanilla ice-cream. Beside the platter was a pitcher of homemade lemonade.

'Is it breakfast time?' asked Tuesday, still holding her father, her eyes shining with happiness.

'It might be,' said Denis. 'It could be lunch or brunch or even dessert. It's hard to tell in the circumstances. But whatever it is, I see, sweet pea, that you're in stark need of significant and substantial sustenance.'

'You came!' Tuesday said again, hugging him even more tightly.

In that long, long hug, Tuesday squeezed in a thousand silent questions and received a thousand inaudible answers.

Eventually Denis said, 'Let's not let the pancakes get cold.'

Reluctantly Tuesday relinquished her grasp on him, and together they sat down at the table and began to eat.

Chapter Twenty-six

If you are lucky enough to live with a dog, then you will almost certainly have spent some time watching your dog dream. There they lie, fast asleep, their closed eyelids trembling, paws twitching as if they are in hot pursuit of a warthog on a savannah, or a cat down an alley, or perhaps – in the manner of dreams – a hamburger on a skateboard.

As was her habit, Apache had stretched out on a cowhide rug on the floor of the Conservatory to sleep while the Gardener attended to routine maintenance. He sat hunched over on his high stool, peering down into a world that lay open for inspection on his workbench, scanning the entire scene within the globe, then flicking a couple of levers on the complicated multi-focal magnifying spectacles in order to examine the details more closely. Meanwhile, Apache – deep in sleep – curled back her lip a little and gave a small yip. The Gardener glanced over at her fondly before turning back to the world he was working on. Inside it was an enormous and very old house with stone walls, a slate roof and a number of chimneys. Around the edges of this enormous house were gardens: formal gardens, vegetable gardens, orchards and flower gardens full of wonderful scents. There was also a walled garden, but it didn't look as if anybody had tended to it for the longest time. The Gardener had only to observe the tangle of overgrown vines to feel his green-tinged thumbs tingle. But he knew to leave the walled garden well alone.

Instead, he levered the entire roof off the great house and lay it down on the bench top. Just as if he'd taken the lid of a doll's house, he was now staring down into all of the mansion's many rooms. It was early morning in this world, and in one bedroom, a lonely girl sat – as if frozen in time – with a breakfast tray in front of a fire that didn't give out nearly enough heat. The Gardener reached in with a tiny fire poker and stirred the coals before adding a few tiny logs of wood.

'There now,' he said, satisfied.

In another bedroom, a lonely boy lay in his bed. The Gardener inspected the fire in the boy's room and saw that it was perfectly well tended. He replaced the roof and surveyed the garden again. He rifled through his collection of paintbrushes until he found one with an almost impossibly fine tip. He dabbed it into a pot of vibrant vermilion paint. He touched it to the feathered breast of a tiny bird that was resting on a bough of an overgrown tree in the walled garden, and sat back to admire his handiwork.

It was then that he realised that Apache was no longer dreaming in a happy, cat-chasing kind of way. Rather than giving out tiny yaps of excitement, she was making sad little whines of distress. Her tail was flicking to and fro and all four of her paws were twitching as if she were racing away from the greatest terror she had ever faced.

As the Gardener watched, Apache snapped open her eyes and lifted her head. Then she was on her feet, her ears pricked, tilting her head from side to side as if trying to tune in to a very faraway noise

'You all right there, girl?' the Gardener asked in concern, but Apache paid him no heed. She only stared up into the darkness above the Conservatory, threw back her head and began to howl. It was a howl like no other the Gardener had ever heard his dog make, and it caused a nasty shudder to run down the length of his spine.

'What is it, girl? Hmm?' the Gardener asked, concerned. 'Apache?'

But she seemed not to hear him, so intent was she on peering up into the worlds.

'What can you hear? What is it, girl?'

The Gardener, too, cocked his head and stared up into the sky, but his dull human ears were not nearly acute enough to pick up the sound that Apache could hear, which was the faraway howling of Baxterr. But although the Gardener could not hear Baxterr's howl, he suddenly did hear a noise much closer at hand: the rattling of clattering crockery. At the end of his workbench a teacup was turned upside down on a saucer. Both the cup and the saucer were shimmying together so violently that the Gardener thought they might rattle themselves clean off the edge of his bench.

Apache bounded across the room and sniffed at the teacup and saucer, then fixed the Gardener with a plaintive look.

'Rooof, rooof, rooof,' she said, urgently.

'You want to go for a walk? That's what all this hullabaloo is about?'

'Rooof,' said Apache, shaking her head.

Then something in the sky caught her eye and she changed her tone, letting out a volley of deep, doorbell barks, insisting for all she was worth that something was coming.

The Gardener slid his magnifying glasses up onto his forehead and followed Apache's gaze. Indeed something was coming. Someone was coming. Someone familiar. A furred creature, tall and dark, was clutching at the railing of a platform that the Gardener recognised as the very same platform that rightly belonged in the Library. And this platform was coming in to land on his cowhide rug.

'Well, I'll be ...' said the Gardener.

'Rooof, rooof,' said Apache to Colette.

'Thank goodness I'm here, indeed,' said Colette Baden-Baden to the dog in her deep, gravelly voice. Then, to the Gardener, she said, 'I thought I was going to be flying around forever. This writing business is far harder than I thought. There must be millions of worlds, and to think I thought I could just find one. I've been out there for hours, searching for the world of Vivienne Small, which is worse than looking for a thimble in a barnyard. And then, I thought maybe the world of Vivienne Small might be still on your desk. I thought you were sending it back out, but perhaps you were delayed. So then I had the job of finding you again. Finally I remembered that you are south if the Library is north. And to my surprise, and enormous relief, here you are!'

'I would call that a mighty bit of navigating,' said the Gardener. He smoothed back his hair, wiped his hands on a handkerchief from his back pocket and indicated the couch beside the ottoman where Colette had fallen not so long ago.

'Coffee?' he asked. This made it seem as if he had guests all the time, whereas the only visitor other than the Librarian that had ever arrived at the Conservatory since he'd taken up his post as the Gardener was Colette Baden-Baden.

'I do not think I have time for coffee,' said Colette. 'I am terribly worried I will be too late to be any use at all. I am woefully bad at this godmothering business. In truth, I am a little embarrassed to realise I don't know how to take responsibility for anyone other than myself.'

The Gardener nodded warily as if he didn't agree, but before he could say anything, Colette continued.

'I apologise for disturbing you twice in such a short time, Silver Nightly, but as you know I promised to take care of Tuesday. After we left here, we did as you suggested, but that Librarian was, let us say, reluctant to help. Baxterr departed from the Library promising to return quickly with news, but alas, he did not. I waited for a very long time. Luckily, while I was waiting, I came across a writer who alerted me to the existence of this platform.'

'Not a tall, gangly kind of fellow by any chance?' asked Silver Nightly, with a twinkle in his eye. 'On the young side?'

'Indeed he was,' said Colette. 'This place, I am discovering, is full of people with great affection for my goddaughter. Unfortunately, the young man was prevented from assisting me further. I took flight – not easily, I have to say. But at last, I got the hang of *that*,' she said, indicating the platform still parked on the rug, quivering a little as if in anticipation of another flight soon. 'So, do you still have the world of Vivienne Small here?'

Silver Nightly sighed and shook his head. 'It's been returned. If I'm not mistaken, I see it right over there.'

Colette followed the direction in which Silver Nightly was pointing. 'Well then, I will be off,' she said.

'Rooof, rooof, rooof,' said Apache, who had been waiting patiently to have her say.

Colette's eyes lit up. 'Are you sure it was him? No other dog?'

'Rooof,' Apache began, and then continued to explain the situation fully to Colette.

'I see. Then there is not a single moment to lose,' said Colette to Apache. She turned to Silver Nightly and said, 'She tells me you have a small world here that contains dogs?'

Silver Nightly frowned, but he nevertheless pointed to the end of his workbench, where the teacup was still jiggling on its saucer. As many of you will remember, this was the very teacup in which the previous Gardener had kept the world of dogs.

'Apache must go there without delay,' said Colette.

'Rooof,' said Apache, looking from human to human and madly wagging her tail.

'Would you care to enlighten me?' Silver Nightly asked mildly.

'Baxterr has sent out a call,' said Colette. 'It is evidently a very particular howl. It means help is required. Urgent help.'

'Help?' said Silver Nightly.

'Do you have a plank in front of your head? From the Winged Dogs.'

'Rooof, rooof, rooof, rooof,' said Apache, bounding over to the bench and directing her noise very pointedly at the overactive teacup.

'You mean Baxterr needs the Winged Dogs … to go to the world of Vivienne Small?' said Silver Nightly.

'Indeed,' said Colette. 'With great haste.'

'Well then,' said the Gardener, and delicately lifted the teacup by its dainty handle. A tiny world shot out from under the teacup, beating a pair of equally tiny furry wings. The world darted skywards, spinning and expanding. The larger it became, the more clearly Colette could make out the gold and pearlescent marbling on the world's surface. Apache watched keenly as it whirled away from the Conservatory. Without turning her head, she gave a very specific, 'Rooof.'

'What's that?' said the Gardener.

'She said she must travel alone this day,' Colette informed him.

The Gardener frowned and scratched his chin. 'Well, all right then,' he said. 'You take care, girl.'

'Rooof,' said Apache, then she spread her magnificent white wings and soared skywards.

Chapter Twenty-seven

In the time he'd spent at the Conservatory, the new Gardener had come to think of the world of dogs as a personal backyard for himself and Apache, a place for them to take walks and for her to enjoy the company of her own kind. Apache had grown into an excellent Gardener's dog – steady and reliable, and with enough strength and energy to fly the Gardener to the many places that he needed to go. And yet, the minute he let the world of dogs out of its teacup, it was as if Apache was a bouncing puppy all over again. When the salt air of the world of dogs got into her nostrils, there was no holding her back.

In the world of dogs, the weather was, as far as the Gardener had observed, always mild, neither cold nor hot. The sky was the many shades of blue a sky can be, and always richly furnished with the plump, fluffy clouds that the Winged Dogs loved to fly through and hide behind when they were playing their games of aerial hide-and-seek. There were soaring cliffs, craggy outcrops, shallow rivers, tumbling waterfalls, and wide sandy beaches on the edge of a green-blue ocean.

Of course, there were dogs everywhere. Old dogs and young dogs, brown and black and golden and white dogs. On a usual day, there would be dogs flying, dogs rolling on the sand, dogs paddling in the ocean, dogs snoozing in the sun. But today, as Apache came into land, the world of dogs was not the least bit usual. The dogs were not gambolling, or playing – not even the smallest pups. They were all gathered on a long stretch of beach, arranged in a large circle, and looking grave.

Apache entered the circle and barked out a message, strong and clear. One by one, the largest, strongest, fittest and bravest of the Winged Dogs stepped forward.

Back in the Conservatory, as soon as Apache took flight, Colette Baden-Baden moved swiftly towards the Librarian's quivering platform and stepped aboard.

As it lifted off the carpet, she called behind her, 'So, I, too, will be off.'

'Now, just a moment there,' said Silver Nightly, taking his eyes off Apache disappearing into the darkness. 'I darn well meant it when I said that you cannot go into Vivienne Small's world. I don't know how you got around the Librarian, but I sure know that you can't go intervening in writers' worlds.'

He made a surprisingly nimble leap, grabbed the platform and hung on, his fingers gripping the edge for all it was worth. The platform rose, lifting him up off the floor.

Colette forced the platform higher, hoping to shake the Gardener loose, but he hung on, dangling at full stretch, his snakeskin boots kicking about in mid-air.

'Let go, you silly man!' called Colette. 'I would hate to tread on your fingers.'

261

'Nope,' said Silver Nightly. 'I demand, Ma'am, that you come in to land.'

At this point Colette decided that the Gardener was simply the most stubborn person she had ever met. She liked him for it, but not so much that she was prepared to spoil her getaway. She urged the platform higher still. Realising how high he was above the Conservatory, the Gardener's grip faltered and he fell, fortunately landing on his ottoman and saving himself a broken ankle.

Colette once again set her gaze on the world of Vivienne Small, its snow-covered mountains glinting through its polished-glass exterior. But the Gardener was not easily beaten, and raced to his collection of neatly coiled lassos. The previous Gardner might have been good with a boathook, but the current one was good with a rope. He selected one and, quick as a rattlesnake, flung it into the sky above. It was an excellent shot, and the platform, with Colette aboard, was instantly captured. The Gardener reeled in his prize.

'Mr Gardener,' shouted Colette Baden-Baden as she was pulled back into the Conservatory and the platform was forced down to the carpet. 'Do you have all your cups in your cabinet? This is an act of outright …'

But then she seemed to lose all vocabulary and instead fixed him with a distinctly hostile stare. He met her gaze, though it literally took his breath away.

'I must take care of Tuesday,' Colette said, spitting every syllable at him in her heavily accented voice. 'I gave my word and I am always a woman of my word. I have to warn you that I lived for a time with a clan of Scandinavian hunters who have made an art form of the hypnosis of wolves. It works perfectly well on humans. So, Silver Nightly, I am going to the world of Vivienne Small! And nothing you can do will stop me.'

Silver Nightly fixed her with his own particular stare and said, 'Ma'am, I need to warn you that I have lived with the Diné of Four Corners and they have a way of hypnotising snakes. It works equally well on humans, I can assure you. So you may try your Scandinavian mind-tricks, but I do not think you will gain the result you're intending. In fact, you might find yourself trussed up here like a chicken ready for baking until Baxterr comes to find you.'

For a very, very long time, Silver Nightly and Colette Baden-Baden stood in grim concentration, staring into each other's faces and doing all they could to overpower the mind of the other. Then, at long last, Silver Nightly began smiling, and then he chuckled, and Colette chuckled, and they both fell onto the couches and laughed like children who have eaten too much sugar. It was quite some time before they calmed down enough for either of them to speak.

Finally Silver Nightly said, 'You're a helluva woman, Colette. And I know you are hell-bent on getting to Tuesday, but Tuesday is in the middle of a story. She's just doing what writers do every day. I don't like it any more than you that Baxterr has summoned help. Or even that Apache has gone alone and the Winged Dogs are on the move. But there are things at work that are part of the mystery of creative thinking. Soon Tuesday'll have a whole flock of help coming to her ...'

'A purpose,' said Colette. 'A purpose of Winged Dogs. I understand from Apache that this is the correct terminology.'

'Ah,' said Silver Nightly. 'My, it'd be useful to have you visit more often. And quite colourful, I expect. Anyway, what I was about to say is: I'm going to make you an offer. You and I are going to fly there together. You are my visitor, and I am prepared to show you some sights. But we will not intervene in anything that is happening there, do you understand me?'

Colette Baden-Baden blinked and gave a brief nod.

'But you are quite sure I will be able to gain access to the world?' Colette asked. 'I will not bounce off and require rescuing again?'

Silver Nightly scratched his cheek. 'Let me think about that for a moment,' he said.

He went to his hat stand and selected a pair of matching white cowboy hats. Returning, he handed one hat to Colette. 'I think that should do,' he said.

Colette stuffed her racoon hat in one of her large pockets and put the cowboy hat on.

Silver Nightly donned the other. Together, they stepped aboard the platform and Colette steered them up into the sky and towards the world of Vivienne Small.

'Colette, you never did tell me. How on earth *did* you get the Librarian to loan you this dang platform of hers?' asked Silver Nightly.

'Oh,' said Colette with a small smile. 'That is a story for another day.'

Silver Nightly raised an eyebrow. And she raised an eyebrow back.

'Is the hat strictly necessary?' Colette asked Silver Nightly, as they began to weave through the worlds towards the world of Vivienne Small.

'Not at all,' said Silver Nightly. 'As the Gardener you get certain privileges. I can go anywhere, and take anyone I need to with me. But I liked the idea of you wearing it.'

Colette continued to fly the platform, but if you'd checked, you'd have seen her eyes smiling.

Chapter Twenty-eight

Serendipity Smith slammed the door of the Librarian's office and strode across the foyer. She was intending to return to the boatshed, but then she stopped in the middle of the wide expanse of floor.

'This isn't right,' she muttered to herself. 'Not right at all.'

Serendipity didn't want to intervene in Tuesday's story, but at the same time she had a dreadful feeling. She couldn't shake it. The hair on her arms was up, and the skin on her back had gone cold.

Without quite even deciding to do it, she found

herself slipping along a hallway and entering a room she had only visited once before, a very long time ago. Inside were shelves exactly like the shelves of the great book room, but the books in this room were quite different. These books were under construction. They were incomplete, unfinished, half done, a quarter done, almost done, or just beginning. But books they were. They shimmered and wobbled. They were diaphanous, pearlescent, watery, waxen. Many of them glowed, others were as translucent as water. Some of them were opaque, and the colour of butterfly wings. Some of them looked as if they would float away or melt if touched, and others vibrated as if they had a tiny beating heart inside them.

Serendipity walked along the rows until she got to M for McGillycuddy. She wasn't at all sure this was a good idea, but at the same time, she felt she had very few options. It was clear that Tuesday was in the world of Vivienne Small. *Their* world. It would be terrible to disturb her if everything was fine, but Serendipity had learned over the years not to ignore her instincts. They were a far more reliable source of information than what appeared to be the facts. All her instincts were telling her to find her daughter.

And there it was. In fact, there *they* were! Three books all bearing the name, in floating, fragile letters – *Tuesday McGillycuddy*. Serendipity felt a thrill of excitement. Her daughter was truly a writer. Here were three books-in-the-making. One was ruby red and looked as if it were made of old-fashioned glass. The second was midnight blue with pale swirls moving through it. It looked rather like it would harden one day and become an exotic and delicious sweet. The third was a shimmer of golden paper fine as cobweb. Again, Serendipity trusted her instincts: she chose the golden one. Ever so gently she slid the book into her hands. It was barely bigger than her palm. The words on its cover moved as if the title was trying to hide from the light. Carefully she attempted to open the book. The pages fluttered as if a breeze had gone through them.

'Hush,' soothed Serendipity. 'It's all right. I just need to see where she is.'

The pages fluttered again, but this time they fluttered to a page at the back of the little volume.

Written there was a tangle of words. They spun about and reorganised themselves and then reorganised themselves again.

'Gently,' said Serendipity. A few words in the middle of the page settled just for a moment.

Down in the garden,
Underneath the tree,
The boy called Loddon
Captured me.

'Oh dear,' said Serendipity. 'Oh dear, oh dear, oh dear.'

She carefully replaced the little book and stood very still for a moment, thinking.

'Right,' she said, having resolved what she must do.

In her office the Librarian was eating raisin toast and drinking tea. She had unscrambled her knit-ting and several balls were newly organised beside her. She glanced up when Serendipity walked in but before she could speak, Serendipity said, in a voice of absolute determination, 'Do not think for a minute I will not go to dramatic lengths to reach my daughter tonight, Madame Librarian. As you know, I have been coming here a long time. And as you also know, I have given the world of writing many days of my life. Days I can never have back. Sunny days, summer days, Saturday afternoons and Sunday mornings, rainy days when my family went to the park and misty days when they played Scrabble. I have given my books days and weeks when I would have preferred to be with my family. But I wrote.

'I have travelled the world for words and reading and imagination. I have been a servant to literature. So now, I am asking you, because I respect you and all you hold dear, to give me a coin so I can find my daughter. Because for once there is nothing you can say that will convince me that I need to put a story first.'

The Librarian said nothing. She simply put a hand into her pocket and handed Serendipity a single coin with a lion's head on one side and a mountain on the other.

With that, Serendipity opened the French doors

of the Librarian's office and stepped out onto the balcony. She walked to the binoculars and put the coin in the slot. At first there was only fog, and then the fog cleared and she could see into the world of Vivienne Small. She saw the deep frost that lay on the fields that led to the Peppermint Forest. She saw the River of Rythwyck frozen solid. She scanned further afield and saw the giant seas that crashed on the shores of the Restless Sea. She saw the Cliffs of Cartavia almost blue with ice. Her eyes travelled further. She saw the Mountains of Margalov and the Purple Desert turned grey with cold. She saw the great crevasse that had split the world in two. She peered down into that crevasse. And then she knew, with all her heart, what she had to do. She had never attempted such a thing before, but with all her instincts humming, she ran down the steps at the side of the balcony. Down, down, down the wide spiral staircase she ran. And when she got to the bottom she found grass and a huge tree, and she thought instantly of the younger Sarah.

What had once been a huge, vaulted cave was partially collapsed. It was still subsiding, even as Serendipity watched. Many of the precarious staircases that crossed the cave this way and that had toppled and broken. It was, Serendipity realised, a cave made of paper. The only light came from a few paper stars and a shred of paper moon hanging high above her. The only sound was that of her footsteps swishing through the tall paper grass. A huge paper sun had fallen to the ground and was glowing only faintly. She propped it up against a broken staircase.

This staircase – like all the others – had been built out of notebooks and writing paper. She pulled one notebook out and recognised her own handwriting. She took in the sheer volume of notebooks and writing and words and ideas and thoughts and stories it had taken to fill every book here. She stared in wonder at this extraordinary place.

'I knew I'd been busy,' she said.

Then she went to the base of the tree. A ladder leaned against it. But it was not upwards that she needed to go. She knelt and pushed aside the paper grass here and there, feeling all about her in the earth. There it was. A trapdoor and a bolt.

'I thought so,' she said.

'Tuesday!' she called. 'Tuesday! I'm coming!'

She slipped back the bolt and pulled up the trapdoor. The most exquisite scent of Denis McGillycuddy's blueberry pancakes floated up to her.

'Tuesday?' she called.

'Mum!' came Tuesday's voice, and as Serendipity dropped herself down into the box, Tuesday flung her arms around her mother.

Serendipity saw the table and two chairs and the remains of a lamp-lit meal. Cups, cutlery and two plates, a jug freshly emptied of its contents save for a few lemon slices, the plates with only a smear of maple syrup remaining.

'He was here?' said Serendipity.

'Things were getting desperate,' said Tuesday.

Serendipity laughed and pulled Tuesday in for another hug.

'Oh, my darling daughter,' she said. 'What a wonderful imagination you have!'

'I think,' said Tuesday, 'that I've done enough for now. I'd like to go home.'

'That is also a wonderful idea,' said Serendipity.

Chapter Twenty-nine

Tuesday emerged from the box and scrambled out underneath the tree, Serendipity following her with the lamp held high. Tuesday squinted into the dimness and took in the fallen staircases, the broken earth and the huge landslide on one side of the cave.

'The tunnel!' she said. 'That's where the tunnel was! How are we going to get out?'

'Oh dear,' said Serendipity. 'I think this is your story, so you are going to have to … oh—'

Tuesday whirled around to see what her mother was staring at.

It was Loddon. He was emerging from a hole

he had made in the wall. Though he was dripping wet, his hair was as bright as ever. As Serendipity and Tuesday watched, stunned, Loddon tried to brush earth and paper from his clothes and out of his bright green hair. This wasn't particularly successful as it was quite clear that he was wet through.

'Sodden Loddon,' Tuesday whispered, and Serendipity smiled.

Loddon took in the destruction the earthquake had wreaked, then peered through the half-light at Tuesday and Serendipity.

'Writer? Are you going somewhere?' he asked.

He came closer, his eyes moving from Tuesday to Serendipity and back again. He paused and frowned. And then he laughed long and loudly.

'Two writers! How brilliant! Little writer, big writer! Oh, the stories will never end. They'll go on and on and on.'

And then he took an even closer look at Serendipity.

'Hello, Loddon,' she said. 'You have been causing a lot of problems. Did you lock up my daughter?'

Loddon stiffened. 'Your *daughter*? No, truly? She is ...? It was you? It is you! My, you got old! Ha ha ha ha ha! It really is you! *My writer.* That's why she didn't know the stories! Ha!'

Tuesday grimaced and leaned closer to her mother.

'But maybe I prefer her. Maybe we'll put you in a box and leave you there, like you did to me!' As he said this, Loddon grew bigger. He shook himself, sending out a spray of water. He was dry again, his green hair upright and swaying.

Tuesday squeezed her mother's hand and backed away against the tree. She could feel the ladder propped there. She grasped it.

'Oh, yes. You'll do fine down there,' said Loddon, pushing Serendipity back towards the open trapdoor. 'We'll get you out from time to time if things get boring. Oh, your daughter can be very entertaining. She gave me a giant and we caused an earthquake! Look at what I can do! We could have you rebuild the staircases. Make you our servant ... Oh, we're going to have fun with you!'

Whack went the ladder, into Loddon. Tuesday swung it with all her might and it took Loddon quite unawares, knocking him to the ground.

'Run!' said Serendipity to Tuesday, throwing down the lantern and pointing to the nearest staircase.

They ran, but behind them the flame from the discarded lantern caught the paper grass and the paper flowers. In a moment, Loddon's feet were also burning. He leapt up and stamped about, then he batted at the fire on his feet with his hands. Then they too were alight.

'Put it out!' screeched Loddon, jumping about, but the more he danced and batted at the flames, the more the sparks flew around him.

'Put it out!' he cried in rage. 'You can't kill me! You will never kill me!'

Flames were licking against the low branches of the tree and running through the grass to the edges of the huge cavern. They were creeping up the staircases and spreading up the sides of the cavern. Tuesday took the staircase two steps at a time. She wasn't even thinking about her fear of heights, only concentrating on getting away from the flames, which were running in bright seams all about the cave.

'I'm right behind you!' called Serendipity. 'Just keep going.'

Up they scrambled. At the first gap in the steps, Tuesday had a moment of hesitation before she leapt across and Serendipity followed. At the next gap they leapt again. Looking down Tuesday could see Loddon running around the tree, still screeching and batting at himself, a dark silhouette against the spectacular display of red and orange that was the magnificent tree fully ablaze. The heat in the cavern was intensifying and the light had grown eerily red. Tuesday could hardly see for smoke. Serendipity began coughing.

'Cover your mouth and nose,' she said to Tuesday, pulling her own T-shirt up over her face so that only her eyes were visible. Tuesday did the same then turned to go higher, but after only a few more steps, she came to a yawning gap between the staircase and a cave in the wall beyond.

'We'll have to jump,' Tuesday said.

'It's too far,' said Serendipity, grabbing Tuesday's arm. 'Think of something else.'

But before she could have another single thought, the roof of the cavern started falling in. Tuesday and Serendipity flattened themselves on the stairs as chunks of earth, paper, sand and rocks fell past them, down into the cavern. Serendipity drew Tuesday closer to her, shielding her from the raining debris. They clung to each other and closed their eyes. Tuesday was sure that at any moment the staircase would tear away from the cavern wall and they would topple far into the fire below, the rock and sand and earth following them.

We'll be buried alive, Tuesday thought.

But then Tuesday could feel a breeze on her face. She opened her eyes and peeked out from under her mother's arm. She saw that the smoke was spiralling up and out, through an opening, and there above them was a circle of pale sky. All around the edges of the widening hole that was appearing in the roof of Loddon's cavern were scrabbling ... paws. Yes, they were paws — enormous paws, clawing away at the earth. And as Serendipity and Tuesday watched, the hole grew larger and larger.

Soon the paws were replaced by faces – big, furry faces with wet black noses and brown eyes. There were golden dogs and brown dogs, white and grey and spotted dogs. There were dogs with patches over their eyes and dogs with blazes down their foreheads. And there, in the midst of them all, was Baxterr.

Seeing Tuesday, Baxterr threw back his head and howled, and his cry was echoed by the other dogs.

'Doggo!' Tuesday called, scrambling to her knees. Baxterr launched himself down into the cave on outspread wings. Barking joyously, he swooped underneath Tuesday and Serendipity. Tuesday grabbed her mother's hand.

'Jump!' she called, and together they landed on Baxterr's broad shoulders.

Far below, Loddon was shrieking. Tuesday buried her face in the soft fur of Baxterr's neck, and knew that she was safe at last.

'Thank you, doggo,' she said. 'I knew you'd come. I knew it.'

'That was far too close for comfort,' said Serendipity. 'Your readers might die of fright before they get to the end.'

Chapter Thirty

Baxterr landed on the frozen sands of the Purple Desert and Tuesday and Serendipity alighted. They were both smoky and covered in dirt, their faces red from the heat of the fire. Tuesday hugged Baxterr's enormous paw, and worried over his wounds. But Baxterr was so delighted to have found Tuesday again that he seemed to feel no pain.

Then a voice cut through the air.

'Put me down, you great, flying guinea pig!'

It was Loddon, pinned between the white teeth of a Winged Dog that had flown down into the cavern and caught him up, his grassy limbs still burning and smouldering. The dog spat him out, unceremoniously, on the cold sand of the desert, then rolled him over and over with a giant paw until the last of the flames was extinguished.

'How dare you touch me?' he roared, trying to get to his feet. 'Don't you know who I am? I am Loddon, I am Merivane, I am Phandor, I am Windish. I am ...'

'A great big green bully!" said Vivienne Small, stepping forwards.

'Vivienne!' said Tuesday, shocked at the sight of Vivienne's ragged appearance, her damaged wings and the bloodstains seeping through her shirt. 'You're alive!'

'How disappointing,' said Loddon. 'I told you, Vivienne Small, there is no room for you in my story!'

He leapt towards Vivienne with superhuman speed, but a huge white dog with a brown patch over her eye was faster still. It was Apache. Mid-leap, she snapped Loddon up in her jaws and took off high into the sky. Then, as they all watched, she dropped him. Serendipity gasped.

Tuesday watched wide-eyed. They could hear a tiny cry growing louder and louder as he fell. But just when it seemed that Loddon was about to smack into the desert floor, another Winged Dog swooped in and caught him in its teeth, and tossed him through the sky to another dog on the wing. And so this game of catch continued, the dogs flinging Loddon from one to the other, sometimes dropping him from great heights. Serendipity began giggling, and then Tuesday and Vivienne joined in. Baxterr barked in agreement. Eventually the dogs returned Loddon to the ground. He was deeply subdued.

'Stop,' Loddon pleaded on his hands and knees, his breath coming in gasps. 'Please make them stop. I'll be good. I'll go back to my box. Just let me go back in my box.'

And this was the scene that met Colette Baden-Baden and Silver Nightly when they flew in over the Purple Desert and landed their platform beside Tuesday, Vivienne, Serendipity and Baxterr.

'Colette!' said Tuesday and Serendipity together.

'Rooof, rooof,' said Apache, and at the sound of her bark, all the other dogs turned to stare at the woman in the great bear coat.

'Wuff, wuff, ruff, ruff, rooof rooof, yip yip, wooff, wooff, gruff gruff,' said the Winged Dogs.

'Goodness! Not all of you at once!' said Colette, laughing.

'Colette, you found us! Hello, Silver Nightly! You're just in time!' said Tuesday.

'I'm so sorry not to get here sooner—' Colette began.

But Serendipity took her hand and said, 'You are here at the perfect time. As always.'

'You are,' agreed Tuesday, hugging her.

Silver Nightly gave Tuesday a wink, and Serendipity a nod.

'It's a great pleasure to meet you in person, Ms Smith,' he said.

Serendipity bowed. 'We are honoured to have the Gardener visit this world. As you can see, I've made rather a mess of it. Can I discuss that with you later? Meanwhile, we have some pressing business to attend to.'

She indicated the dishevelled creature on the grey sand. Colette took a good look at him. Though he appeared to have once been green, his hair, feet and hands were blackened, and he appeared to be suffering from shock.

'And what is this?' she asked.

'This is Loddon,' Tuesday replied.

'He has gotten far too big for his boots,' said Serendipity. 'It's my fault. I needed him, when I was very small. He was my only friend and he loved my stories. I wrote everything for him, so he would never be hungry. Or so I would never be hungry, I think. Somehow I wrote my hunger into him and then he became something else. Frightening. I buried him under the tree in our backyard and tried to forget about him. I never imagined he'd grow so big and strong down there under the earth.'

'That's what comes of burying your fears,' said Colette. 'They like to resurface at the worst possible moment.'

Silver Nightly bent and inspected the grassboy. Then, with care, he pulled a length of rope from his pocket and trussed Loddon's hands and feet.

'Let's not take any chances,' he said. 'I can tell a coyote when I see one.'

'Now what do we do with him?' Tuesday asked.

'We give him a serious talking-to,' said Serendipity.

'Story time, Loddon,' said Tuesday.

Loddon looked up, startled. He began to speak, but Serendipity put a finger to his mouth.

'You start, Tuesday,' she said. 'In my experience, words are more powerful than anything else.'

In a quiet voice, and staring right into Loddon's eyes, Tuesday said:

Down in the cavern, beside the paper tree,
A boy called Loddon captured me.
He decided he would keep me there,
Inside his pretty paper snare.
He appeared at first to be strong and tall,
But inside a bully is someone small,
And though they cannot help but speak,
You'll find that what they say is weak.

Tuesday glanced at her mother and Serendipity winked at her. Loddon's eyes widened and he tried to cry out, but his voice had gone thin and wobbly. And not only that, he was shrinking. Right before their eyes, he was growing smaller, rolling around on the sand as if in agony. The ropes about his feet and hands had slipped off him, but he didn't seem to notice. Instead he writhed and groaned as if the words were damaging him much more savagely than flames or cross-bolts. Then Serendipity knelt beside him, speaking softly.

There once was a grassboy who lived by a tree,
I wove him together to comfort me.
But all he wanted was fame and glory,
He forgot he was a friend in a story.
Goodbye, little grassboy, growing very small.
Soon, in a moment, you'll be hardly here
    at all.

'No!' squeaked Loddon. 'I'll be good ...'
But he was no bigger than a wooden spoon now, and they could barely hear him.

Then Vivienne knelt down and said, quite gleefully:

Little Loddon grassboy, where will you go?
Grown so small and tiny-oh,
We could put you in a jar with the lid on
*   tight,*
And I'd have to say it would serve you right.
I never really liked you, not from the start,
But that was because you smelled like a fart.

Tuesday and Vivienne giggled. Serendipity and Colette chuckled, and Silver Nightly raised his eyebrows. The dogs, sitting in a wide circle with the wind ruffling their many-coloured coats, kept their eyes fixed on Loddon. He was so small that he was hardly bigger than a popsicle stick.

Colette drew a small, empty bottle from her pocket. She handed it to Serendipity, who lifted the tiny wriggling Loddon into the bottle and stopped the lid.

Serendipity peered at the little figure inside the bottle and, with a grin at Vivienne, said:

High above the ocean, in a tree house I know,
Lives a girl called Vivienne, with an arrow and
a bow.
If you look upon a shelf, you'll see she keeps
a boy,
In a bottle with a cork, but he is not a toy.
His name is Loddon Grassboy and if you set
him free,
He will wreak a lot of havoc, as you can
plainly see,
So she keeps him in a bottle, and he watches
time go by,
For the heart of a writer can simply never die.

With this, Serendipity handed the bottle to
Vivienne who, without glancing at Loddon, put
him in her pocket.

Observing the blood crusted on Vivienne's
shoulder, her torn and battered wings, and
Baxterr's injuries, Collette said, 'I see that some
of us need a little ointment.'

She pulled out a battered tin and handed it
to Vivienne Small, who opened it, sniffed its
contents, and frowned, but then proceeded to

carefully take a fingerful of the ointment and apply it first to Baxterr's damaged paw and wing, and then to her own shoulder. Tuesday helped by working the ointment into the torn edges of Vivienne's wings. Within a few minutes, the wounds were all remarkably improved.

Vivienne handed back the tin to Colette, but Colette insisted she keep it.

'If that isn't intervening?' she asked the Gardener, but he only winked.

'Helluva woman,' he said under his breath.

'I think it's time to go home,' said Vivienne Small. 'Wouldn't you say, Ermengarde?'

To the surprise of almost everyone, a small black face appeared from under Vivienne's hair.

'Well, who's a clever girl, then?' Tuesday said, reaching out to scratch the rat's pointed chin. 'I didn't know where you'd gone, but I see you found your way home.'

'Home,' said Serendipity, with a sigh. 'Yes. But before we go, could I have a word with you, dear Gardener?'

Together, Serendipity and Silver Nightly took a stroll across the desert, their heads bowed.

At last, they shook hands and returned to the group.

'Well, I'll be going,' said Silver Nightly. Apache stood beside him in her huge dog form. 'It's been an honour to visit with you all. And to meet you, Ms Baden-Baden, most especially,' he said, shaking Colette's hand. 'I think you'll be needing to take back this here platform to a certain Librarian. Unless, of course, you would like a means to come visit me again?'

Colette blushed. It went from her chin to her forehead. Serendipity couldn't be sure if it was the idea of returning the platform, Silver Nightly's handshake, or his invitation that had caused this effect. But something about it made Serendipity smile.

'I'm not so very sure the Librarian will be wanting to see me again,' said Colette gruffly.

'I could be the one to take the platform back,' suggested Tuesday.

Baxterr nuzzled Tuesday.

'I know, doggo,' Tuesday said. 'And I don't want to be without you another minute either. But I think Mum and Colette need to get home.

How about I'll take this back to the Library and then you come to get me?'

'Ruff,' agreed Baxterr.

'No adventures along the way,' said Colette.

'No adventures along the way,' said Tuesday, grinning. 'I promise!'

Then the Winged Dogs all barked together.

'They are leaving,' said Colette.

'Thank you!' said Serendipity. 'It was lovely to see you all again!'

'Thank you!' said Tuesday. 'You were brilliant!'

The dogs all howled and in a flurry of furred wings, they took flight. And Silver Nightly, Apache, Colette, Baxterr, Tuesday, Vivienne and Serendipity watched until they were out of sight.

'A purpose of Winged Dogs,' said Silver Nightly. 'Well I'll be ...'

Chapter Thirty-one

Back in the Conservatory, Apache lay on a rug before the fire. A fresh pot of coffee steamed on the hearth, and the Gardener – at his bench – was at work. The world of Vivienne Small sat on the stand in front of him, its lid removed. He took a thermometer out of a jar on his workbench and shook the mercury down. Then he laid one end of the thermometer against the slopes of the Mountains of Margalov.

'Sure is cold,' he murmured.

He dipped the thermometer into the Restless Sea, but the reading was barely any higher. He reached under the bench and hunted around for a Bunsen burner, which he slid underneath the freezing cold world. He turned on the gas, lit the burner with a match and turned the flame down as low and soft as it would go.

Next he got to work repairing a big split in the earth, and filling in an enormous hole. He worked, deep in concentration, for a long time. Then he sat back, pushed his magnifying glasses up onto his head, and smiled with satisfaction.

'Well, little world,' said the Gardener fondly. 'How does that feel?'

It felt wonderful. When the world of Vivienne Small was catapulted back out into the sky, it looked and felt like a completely different place. The sands of the Purple Desert were once again bright and glowing. Ice had calved away from the Cliffs of Cartavia. The River of Rythwyck had thawed and sunshine was glinting off its deep blue waters. The hands on the clocks in the City of Clocks were no longer frozen stuck, and – in a rare moment of synchronicity – every clock chimed the same hour. The people of the city stepped out from their homes to find the streets no longer knee-deep in snow, and the waters of the Letitia Mabanquo fountain were no longer frozen, but spouting and spurting and gurgling. Fruit was ripening on the trees and fish were leaping in the river.

In the air and on the ground, in the sky and amid the trees, from the east to the west, from the north to the south, in every last corner, it was suddenly springtime. Birds smoothed their ruffled feathers and sang songs they had almost forgotten that they knew. Creatures poked their noses out of their holes and homes, and sniffed at scents that they had thought to never smell again. Squirrels were climbing out of their burrows, and butter-flies were emerging from defrosted chrysalises. All through the Peppermint Forest, ferns quivered and trees shivered, all of them glorying in the simple fact of life returning.

Chapter Thirty-two

You will be pleased to learn that when Tuesday returned the platform to the great Library (Colette having informed her, rather reluctantly, of all she had done) the Librarian was not so very cross as might have been expected. In fact, she was even forced to acknowledge that Colette had been an essential part of Tuesday's story. She did not, however, entirely forgive the sarsaparilla splashes on her chaise longue.

Serendipity and Colette returned to Brown Street. That very day they began the process of cleaning the tall, narrow house from top to bottom, and chasing as much of the sadness out

297

as they possibly could. Within a few days there was clean washing in the drawers, fresh flowers on the table and all manner of food in the cupboards and the refrigerator. The blinds and curtains were open again, sunlight was streaming in the windows and there was music playing. A large photo of Denis hung in the front hall, and Serendipity smiled at it each time she passed.

Up in her writing room, her old typewriter was waiting faithfully on the freshly polished desk, and a stack of crisp, white paper rested right beside it. Serendipity felt a familiar tingle in the tips of her fingers and in the corners of her mind.

'Yes,' she whispered to herself, 'it's time.'

And where was Tuesday? Well, Baxterr rejoined her in the world of Vivienne Small, carrying with him a letter from Serendipity in which she suggested that Tuesday and Vivienne take a small holiday while Brown Street underwent a spring clean. And so Tuesday stayed on at Vivienne's tree house. Baxterr, of course, had to adopt his small-dog size in the evenings when it was time for him to curl up at the foot of Tuesday's hammock to sleep. But he spent his days at full Winged-Dog stretch, with Tuesday on his back, and Vivienne Small flying along beside them, relishing the wide blue wings that could take her anywhere.

Ermengarde chose not to join them. It seemed she had had quite enough of adventuring for a time, and was perfectly pleased to stay at home exploring the delights of the tree house – and from time to time keeping a watchful eye on Loddon, whom Vivienne had placed on a high shelf still neatly and firmly stoppered in Colette's bottle.

Tuesday and Vivienne's springtime days were full of visits with Vivienne's unusual friends, who were scattered throughout the world of Vivienne Small. They took a balloon trip in the foothills of the Mountains of Margalov, a fishing trip on the Mabanquo River, a stroll through the Golden Valley, and a sailing adventure aboard *Vivacious II*. They also visited some of Vivienne's other homes. One evening, when Baxterr was snoring, and Tuesday and Vivienne were roasting freshly caught red-jackets on the campfire at the mouth of Vivienne's cave home, Vivienne asked, 'What exactly is a writer?'

Tuesday swallowed.

'A writer?' she repeated. 'Um …'

In all the time she had known Vivienne, she had managed to avoid talking about this in any detail. For some reason, she had never wanted to tell Vivienne that she was, well, a character in a book.

Tuesday tried again, 'A writer is someone who … writes books.'

'Yes, obviously,' said Vivienne, giving Tuesday a light punch on the arm. 'But why did Loddon call you *his* writer? And *my* writer? What's that all about?'

Tuesday took a deep breath.

'He thought I was my mother. When she was a girl. Apparently my mother and I look alike, except for the colour of our hair.'

'But it still doesn't make sense,' said Vivienne.

'Well … you know how I live in a different world from you?'

'Yes,' said Vivienne.

'So,' said Tuesday, 'in my world, my mum, well … she writes books. Books that everybody reads. That everyone loves.'

'Books about what?' Vivienne asked.

'Well, when she first started writing, she wrote about Loddon. But then she grew up and started writing books about a girl called Vivienne Small,' Tuesday said. 'About you.'

Vivienne frowned as she removed her skewered fish from the fire.

'Me? How did she know about me?'

'I guess she just imagined,' said Tuesday.

'Oh, I see,' Vivienne said, then blew on the fish and tore off a small piece. 'Yum. That's ready!'

Tuesday waited for more questions, but they did not come. They ate their red-jackets and talked about stars. And Vivienne Small did not mention the topic of writers again.

One evening, Tuesday and Vivienne (with Ermengarde on her shoulder), were standing at the railing of the tree house watching Baxterr zoom through the sky over the Restless Sea. They were admiring how his winged form made beautiful shadows on the water in the pewter-coloured twilight, when a mauve pigeon alighted on the railing right beside them. It cooed self-importantly, and puffed out its feathery chest.

Attached to one of its legs, with a length of narrow purple ribbon, was a small scroll. Vivienne untied it. The pigeon cooed again, and flew away rather urgently.

'I think it's for you,' Vivienne said, handing the scroll to Tuesday.

It was sealed with purple wax, and in the wax was imprinted a curly letter L. Tuesday broke the seal and read the words written in mauve ink within: *Miss McGillycuddy, to the Library. Say your goodbyes. Make all haste. – L.*

'Does it mean you have to go?' Vivienne asked, looking disappointed.

'I'm afraid so,' said Tuesday.

Tuesday would have liked to hug Vivienne goodbye, but she knew that Vivienne was not exactly the hugging type. So she reached out to gently tug a lock of Vivienne's hair, but Vivienne rushed at her and gave her a quick, strong hug.

'You will be back,' Vivienne announced fiercely.

'Yes,' said Tuesday.

'*When?*' Vivienne demanded.

'Whenever you start a new adventure, Vivienne Small!' said Tuesday, with a grin.

'I'll see you tomorrow, then,' said Vivienne, smiling.

'Maybe not *that* soon,' Tuesday said.

'Well, okay then. How about the day after that?'

Baxterr, hearing Tuesday's call, glided in close to the tree house and hovered beneath the verandah railing to allow Tuesday to lower herself onto his shoulders. He ruffed a goodbye to Vivienne Small, and then swooped back out over the waters of the Restless Sea before carving a beautiful turn over the Peppermint Forest and heading towards the Hills of Mist.

'Goodbye, Tuesday!' Vivienne yelled, waving her arms wildly.

'Goodbye, Vivienne!' Tuesday yelled.

Evening had fallen, and the Librarian was standing on the balcony as Tuesday and Baxterr

approached the gardens of the Library. The
Librarian was wearing a violet gown with a high
ruffle around the neck, and a pair of sparkling
high heels. Every few seconds she peered impatiently into a pair of mounted binoculars.

'Come, come, Ms McGillycuddy, or you'll
miss the whole thing!' the Librarian called, beck-
oning as Baxterr made a comfortable landing on
the mist-shrouded lawn.

'Quickly, child! Or the moment will pass,' the
Librarian said, and Tuesday was astonished by
the soft, almost quavering quality to her voice,
so different from her usual imperious tone. 'Look
through here, dear. I've set the sights for you.
Don't bump anything.'

Tuesday peered into the eyepieces and squinted
a little. She could see a segment of almost-black
sky. But in the middle was a spiral of sparkling
dust particles. It was spinning, and as it spun, its
centre became more solid, and it seemed to draw
in more glittering motes from the air.

'What is it?' Tuesday asked.

'That, my dear, is a world being born,' the Librarian said, with a sigh of emotion. '*Your* world.'

'Really?'

The spiral was tightening into a something more like a hazy, shimmering ball. Tuesday thought that it seemed to be emitting its own light.

'This is a privilege, Tuesday. Rare and precious. Most writers miss the whole thing. Their world forms while they're at home writing, or while they're sleeping, or while they're walking to the bus stop. But you, Tuesday, you are here, upon my balcony watching it happen. Do you know what that means?'

'Not really, Madame Librarian,' Tuesday said.

Tuesday watched the glimmering ball spinning in space.

'What you see is the core of your world. Its very heart. And right now, as it's forming, you may choose what it is that *you* want to place at very centre of your world,' the Librarian said.

'You mean, the way Loddon was the centre of Mum's world?' Tuesday asked.

'Ah, a cautionary tale, right there,' said the Librarian. 'Serendipity was such a very little girl when her world formed. And who happened to be there, at the beginning of it all? Hmm? Who, but a little grassboy who loved her stories and always wanted more.'

'You mean she never got to choose?'

'Hardly any writer gets to make a conscious choice. Most writers' worlds form around whatever is in their heart or mind. And that thing never dies. I did once know a writer, who, just like you, had the opportunity to choose what he kept at the heart of his world.'

'What did he pick?'

'It was a lock of hair,' the Librarian said, blushing and patting her short silver tresses. 'Some writers are terribly romantic. Others write out of wit, or anger, or fear. So do choose wisely, Tuesday. It is entirely your secret. You might make it a thing, or a memory, or a word, or an idea. Or indeed, a person. Anything you like can form the heart of your world. But choose wisely, Tuesday McGillycuddy. I do advise against putting fame or money at the heart of your world. You will find no matter how much you get, it's never enough. Choose something that will nurture and nourish you. Not something fashionable, but something classic. Something that will last your whole life long.'

'I don't know what I have to do, Madame Librarian.'

'Yes you do, Tuesday,' the Librarian said. 'You do it every day.'

'You mean … imagine?'

'Yes, dear.'

And so she did. Tuesday imagined, and her world spun, and grew, gathering layer, upon layer, upon layer. And at its heart, someone was standing in a striped pink-and-white shirt wearing an apron. He was mixing something in a bowl. He waved to Tuesday and – still looking through the binoculars – she waved back. The world kept forming, developing a smooth undulating surface of a landscape waiting to be made. Its creamy-white exterior gave hints of riverbeds and mountain peaks, or perhaps they were cities and towns. It could have been either; it could be anything. This was a world waiting to be furnished, however Tuesday chose.

'Do you like your world? Do you?' the Librarian asked, her eyes a little misty.

'Oh yes,' Tuesday said. 'It's perfect.'

Chapter Thirty-three

At a certain lighthouse at the end of the earth, a radio crackled into life. Beyond the lighthouse window, there was barely a smudge of light in the morning sky, and the choppy surface of the sea was still empty of the day's flotilla of boats.

'Senora Smeet, Senora Smeet,' came a heavily-accented voice. 'Do you copy?'

Miss Digby had been asleep, lying on her back with a sleeping mask across her eyes, her arms folded tidily on her chest atop the covers. At the sound of Constanza's voice, she leapt immediately out of bed in her floral nightie and snatched up the radio transmitter.

'Yes, Constanza. I mean, *sí*, Constanza. Roger that,' she said in a bright and cheerful voice that was meant to indicate that she had certainly not been sleeping so late. *What* time *was it?* she wondered. 'Over,' she added, remembering at last to let go of the transmitter button.

'I have a call for you from Sarah McGeeelly-coddy,' Constanza said. 'Connecting you now. Over.'

'Hello?' came a different voice, a voice that Miss Digby had been waiting months to hear. 'Hello?'

'Hello! Oh, my goodness! Is it truly you? Are you all right? Do you need me?'

'Yes! Yes, and no. No, I just wanted to tell you that I'm home again at Brown Street, and there's nothing to worry about.'

'Home again?' repeated Miss Digby, perplexed. 'But wherever have you been?'

'It's a long story,' Serendipity replied. 'But I also wanted to say thank you, Miss Digby. I cannot thank you enough for everything you've done for me, spending all that time at the end of the earth on my behalf.'

Miss Digby glanced at the large aquarium across the room, where Gerald the lobster was doing an erratic dance with his tentacles and his many legs.

'Don't give it a thought,' said Miss Digby, smiling at Gerald. 'Honestly, it's been no bother at all.'

'I think it's time you took a holiday, Miss Digby.'

'A holiday?'

'Absolutely,' Serendipity said. 'Somewhere warm, with lots of people – art and movies.'

'Aah,' said Miss Digby. 'That's all very well, but ...'

'I insist,' said Serendipity. 'I think I'd like to be myself for a little while. Would that be okay with you?'

'Well of *course*, but what about everything else? The bills? The correspondence? Your schedule? I'm not sure that ...'

'I have one of my oldest friends staying with me. She's here with me right now,' Serendipity said, and if Miss Digby had been able to peer through the radio waves and see into the house at

310

Brown Street, she would have observed Colette Baden-Baden sitting at the kitchen table with a hairbrush, a polystyrene head covered with a wig of long, auburn curls, and a bewildered expression upon her face. 'She's helping me out for the next few weeks while you take some well-deserved time off. Now, I must go, Miss Digby. Thank you again. I couldn't be me without you, you know.'

'Well, goodbye then,' said Miss Digby, somewhat wistfully.

'Goodbye. Over and out.'

Miss Digby replaced the radio handpiece and then her face fell.

'Oh,' she said. 'Oh dear!'

She pulled up a chair to the side of the aquarium tank, sat down and spoke softly against the glass.

'Gerald,' she said. 'Gerald, I don't want you to take it personally, but, well, all good things must come to an end. Today, Gerald, will be our last day together. I'm not sure if it was good for you, but I thought you were wonderful.'

Chapter Thirty-four

Several weeks had passed since Tuesday had returned to Brown Street from the world of Vivienne Small, and in that time, she had been busy at school and busy at home. It was Sunday morning and Tuesday woke up feeling flat. She slipped quietly out of the house and, taking Baxterr, walked the entire length of City Park. She lingered by the lake, and stood by the fountain, and said hello to all her favourite statues. She observed snowdrops and early daffodils that lifted their heads to the light. She felt the sun on her face and her hair blow about in the early sea breeze that whispered through the city. She felt the grass beneath her shoes. In the distance she heard the rumble of traffic.

In the tall apartments on one side of the park Tuesday saw windows glinting, and she tried to imagine who was inside eating eggs and bacon, toast and marmalade or even Colette's idea of breakfast – muesli. She wondered if any of them were making pancakes. She wondered whether she would ever meet anyone else who made polka dot brownies or ham-on-cheese-on-more-cheese toast.

She sat on a park bench and took out a notebook. Baxterr settled at her feet, his ears twitching as he watched ducks paddling about in the early-morning light. The new page in the notebook was perfectly blank. Tuesday smoothed it down and uncapped her black pen.

'Dear Dad,' she wrote, 'I will always think of you at the park throwing the frisbee to Baxterr. I'll always remember you making up rhymes on the walk home. And the way you took my hand as we crossed the street. At night I'll think of you leaving the lamp on and the door open, just the way I used to like it. And the way you always knew what day I needed my sports shoes.'

She continued on for a page or more, noting all the things Denis had done that she would never forget. When she had finished writing, she closed the notebook and capped the pen. She had the feeling that there were many more words to be written about Denis, and that it might take weeks or months or maybe even years to write them all down. But this was enough for now.

'Come on, doggo,' she said, getting to her feet.

As they passed the wishing pond, Tuesday dug a small silver coin from her pocket and flipped it into the water. She didn't stay to watch as it settled to the bottom. If she had, she might have noticed that it sparkled.

As they walked home, she said to Baxterr, 'It will always be different without Dad. But it doesn't mean there won't be great days.'

Baxterr ruffed as if in agreement. As they neared Brown Street, he dashed a little way ahead of Tuesday, his tail wagging and his fur shining in every shade of golden brown. He raced up the steps and waited for Tuesday to open the door. Tuesday climbed the steps. There it was, home. All five storeys of it.

Next door, their neighbour Mr Garfunkle was coming out his front door with Gloria, his new cocker spaniel puppy, leaping in excitement at his feet. Tuesday waved and Mr Garfunkle waved back.

'Some things go on being the same, doggo, and some things don't,' she said.

The front door suddenly swung open and Blake Luckhurst was standing before them.

'Surprise! I came on the early train at Colette's invitation.'

He grabbed Tuesday by the shoulder and gave her a hug as they walked inside.

'Ha, there you are,' said Colette, emerging from the front room. 'Lucky you're not *there*. I was starting to get a little worried. Come, I have a surprise for you.'

In the front room, Colette's many silver suitcases were neatly stacked to one side. Serendipity was sitting on the couch in her pyjamas and dressing-gown. The painting had been removed again from one wall and the projector set-up to face the large white space.

'Sit,' instructed Colette.

As soon as Tuesday and Baxterr had obediently taken their places on the couch beside Serendipity, Colette said, 'Well, we leave you to it.'

'Aren't you going to stay?' asked Serendipity.

'No,' said Colette. 'My assistant chef and I have a very important recipe to create. Breakfast will be served at the end of the screening.'

Tuesday and Serendipity glanced at each other and raised their eyebrows. Serendipity put her arm around Tuesday and pulled her in close. She tapped a button on the remote and the wall lit up.

The words on the screen said: *For Serendipity and Tuesday*. Music began. The first picture was a baby with a curl of dark hair. Serendipity gasped and covered her mouth. Next there was a toddler in blue-and-white-striped shorts and a red t-shirt. And the same boy chewing an enormous biscuit.

'Is that Dad?' Tuesday asked.

'It is,' said Serendipity, holding her daughter tight.

Tuesday began smiling and didn't stop. Here were all the years she had never known her father. Photos and films that she had never seen. Denis as a boy on a three-wheeler bike. Denis holding a teddy bear. Denis dressed up as a cowboy, and beside him a girl dressed as a lion, her arms crossed and her teeth bared. She looked remarkably like Colette.

'Is that …?' whispered Tuesday.

'It is,' replied Serendipity.

There was a young Denis in a school uniform. Denis sleeping under a tree with a book in his hands. Denis as a boy decorating a large square cake. And proudly presenting a tray of chocolate eclairs. Denis with another cake. And another. Denis winning a prize for the best cake. Denis working in a restaurant kitchen. Denis in a tuxedo. Denis shaking hands with two people who appeared to be famous. Denis standing outside a restaurant beside a very tall girl. Tuesday stared.

'It's Colette again!' she gasped.

Serendipity was crying, but she was laughing too.

And then came Denis with Serendipity on a couch. Denis beside a woman holding a pot plant in an elaborate macramé holder who Tuesday knew from photographs was Serendipity's mother. Serendipity and Denis with a bearded man who Tuesday knew had been Denis's father. There were Denis and Serendipity amid a gaggle of people who might have been friends or cousins and a sign in the background saying *Sweet Cactus*. Serendipity at work on an old-fashioned type-writer. Serendipity asleep with a book still open on her pyjamas.

Then came a wedding with Serendipity in a bright orange dress with bright orange shoes and Denis in a pink suit cutting a cake covered in flowers. And then Denis and Serendipity on a yacht, then on camels, then on elephants. Denis and Serendipity wearing scuba diving equipment, together with Colette. All of them on skis with a huge snow-capped mountain behind them. And then at last there was Brown Street with a SOLD sticker on the estate agent's sign on the fence.

There was an image of Serendipity pregnant and then a little bit more pregnant and then heavily pregnant. Serendipity holding a brand-new baby in her arms. Serendipity with the baby asleep on her lap as she typed at an old-fashioned typewriter.

Serendipity grasped Tuesday's hand and they held one another tightly as the images kept coming. Here was Denis sleeping with a tiny baby on his chest. The baby being washed in the kitchen sink. Soon the baby had fairy floss hair and was sitting up and chewing a board book. The baby was in a high-chair eating what looked like tuna mornay. And then watermelon. And a mango. And cake with a single candle. There was Denis taking her hands to help her walk across the floor. Then he was holding her on a tiny tricycle and running her down the hallway to Serendipity. And holding her hands as she lifted a tiny foot in the sea. And helping her blow out two candles on a cake in the shape of a blue balloon.

There was Serendipity holding a bottle of champagne in one hand and a book called *I Know about Vivienne Small* in the other. And Tuesday was being thrown up in the air by Denis.

Tuesday, Denis and Serendipity were running in the park together. Tuesday and Denis at the stove together in the kitchen. And Denis and Serendipity holding the small Tuesday between them as they stood on the doorstep of Brown Street waving goodbye.

The images faded and words appeared. They read: *Sometimes we get very lucky with the people we love.* The music continued and then faded away. Tuesday wiped away tears and Serendipity did the same, and then they hugged each other tighter and cried some more. Suddenly, over Serendipity's shoulder, Tuesday saw Denis sitting in the chair by the window. He turned and smiled at her.

Tuesday smiled back, and then watched the image of her father fade into the shadows.

'What?' asked Serendipity.

'Oh, I just saw him,' said Tuesday. 'Dad.'

'Yes,' said Serendipity, 'I've seen him too. It's somehow reassuring, knowing he's still here with us sometimes, even if it's not at all the same.'

From the kitchen the most amazing smell drifted into the room. Tuesday breathed deeply.

'Well,' said Colette, looking in. 'Breakfast.'

And so we leave them at Brown Street – Tuesday, Colette, Serendipity, Blake and Baxterr. It isn't perfect. Life never is. There will be weather we hadn't expected, disappointments and catastrophes. There will be fun and beauty and wonder, too, and mysteries we could never have imagined. And if we're very lucky, there will be many days with people we love, friends at the table and blueberry pancakes forever.

THE END

ACKNOWLEDGEMENTS

WE WOULD LIKE TO THANK ALL six of our children for their enthusiasm for words, stories and books, including ours. We thank them for tolerating us on those occasions when we are vague or preoccupied, and for understanding that we sometimes have one foot in another world.

We would also like to acknowledge the young readers who have enjoyed and embraced Tuesday's first two adventures. We have met some of you in classrooms, libraries and book-shops. Others of you have sought us out. Your drawings, letters, questions, observations and Book Week costumes have touched us deeply, and they have also enriched the worlds of Tuesday McGillycuddy and Vivienne Small. Especially, we thank Lawrence Jeffs, Grace Middleton, Heidi Bedloe, Charmian Wallman and Matilda Verdon-Black for reading this book in manuscript form and sharing their marvellously insightful responses.

Thanks go to our publishers – Allen & Unwin in Australia, Magellan in Germany, and Henry Holt in the USA – for championing our books from beginning to end. And, as ever, we are grateful to our parents and extended families for supporting us, making the writing life so much easier.

Our wonderful husbands, John and Rowan, have done wonders, from writing songs about Tuesday that have been sung at our launches to making life-sized papier-mâché vercaka. We thank them for being part of Tuesday's story.

And lastly, we would like to thank each other. To collaborate in the personal, mysterious business of writing fiction is both a challenge and a risk. We would like to thank each other for meeting that challenge with courage, for filling the gaps in each other's areas of expertise, and – perhaps most importantly – for the friendship, the laughter and the chocolate custard.

A NOTE FROM ANGELICA BANKS

IN WRITING THE TUESDAY MCGILLY-cuddy Adventure series, we have drawn deeply on our love of children's literature. In the pages of our books are the hints and echoes of the books listed here. But you might also find traces of other books, for it is the way of stories to talk to each other across the years.

Swallows and Amazons by Arthur Ransome
The Secret Garden by Frances Hodgson Burnett
The Chronicles of Narnia by C.S. Lewis
Peter Pan by J.M. Barrie
Guess Who My Favourite Person Is by Byrd Baylor
The Blue Balloon by Mick Inkpen
The Faraway Tree series by Enid Blyton
The Old Man and the Sea by Ernest Hemingway
Charlotte's Web by E.B. White
A Tale of Two Cities by Charles Dickens
Carbonel by Barbara Sleigh
The Hobbit by J.R.R. Tolkien
Everything ever written by Roald Dahl
The poetry of Hilaire Belloc

Angelica Banks is not one writer but two. Heather Rose and Danielle Wood have been friends for years and each of them has written award-winning books for adults. When they decided to write together for younger readers, they chose a pen name to make things easy. They live in Tasmania, an island blessed with wonderful stories and beautiful clouds.

Blueberry Pancakes Forever is the third book in the Tuesday McGillycuddy series. While writing this book, Danielle and Heather took long walks on beaches and drank endless cups of tea. Sometimes they laughed and sometimes they cried, because writing is like that.

www.tuesdaymcgillycuddy.com